Sofia F

Sofia Petrovna

Lydia Chukovskaya

TRANSLATED BY ALINE WERTH

Emended by Eliza Kellogg Klose

NORTHWESTERN UNIVERSITY PRESS

EVANSTON, ILLINOIS

Northwestern University Press
www.nupress.northwestern.edu

First published in English as *The Deserted House*. Copyright © 1967 by E. P. Dutton & Co., Inc., and Barrie and Rockliff. Northwestern University Press emended paperback edition published 1988 by arrangement with E. P. Dutton, a division of NAL Penguin Inc. Reprinted by arrangement with Dutton, an imprint of Penguin Publishing Group, a division of Penguin Random house LLC. All rights reserved.

Printed in the United States of America

15   14   13   12

ISBN 978-0-8101-1150-9

Library of Congress Cataloging-in-Publication Data

Chukovskaia, Lidiia Korneevna.
    [Sof'ia Petrovna. English]
    Sofia Petrovna / Lydia Chukovskaya ; translated by Aline Werth ; emended by Eliza Kellogg Klose.
        p. cm.
    Originally published: The deserted house. New York : Dutton, 1967.
    ISBN 0-8101-1150-0 (alk. paper : pbk.)
    1. Soviet Union—History—1925–1953—Fiction. I. Werth, Aline II. Chukovskaia, Lidiia Korneevna. Deserted house. III. Title.
PG3476.C485S5813 1994
891.73'42—dc20   94-2490
                                                                          CIP

Contents

Author's Note

THE story now seeking the attention of readers was written twenty-two years ago, in Leningrad, in the winter of 1939–1940. In it I attempted to record the events just experienced by my country, my friends, and myself. I could not refrain from writing about them, though I had, of course, no hope of seeing the story in print. I had little hope even that the school exercise book containing the clean copy of it would escape destruction and be preserved. It was dangerous to keep it in the drawer of my desk, but I couldn't bring myself to burn it. I regarded it not so much as a story as a piece of evidence, which it would be dishonorable to destroy.

The war came. The siege of Leningrad came and ended. The people keeping the exercise book perished, but the book itself survived. Having left Leningrad a month before the war began, I spent the years 1941–1944 far away from my native city, and it was only at the end of the war that my exercise book, after a long absence, miraculously returned to me. The war ended. Stalin died. More and more I began to entertain the hitherto impossible hope that a time was coming when my story might see the light of day.

After the speeches made at the Twentieth and Twenty-second Party Congresses, pointing to a better present and denouncing the darker aspects of the past, I became more anxious than ever that my story should be made available to readers and so serve to further a cause which I regard as vitally important: in the name of the future, to help to reveal the causes and the consequences of the great tragedy the people had suffered. I have no doubt that literature will turn often to the subject of the thirties, that writers

1

in possession of far more facts than I had at the time, as well as greater analytic skill and greater artistic talent, will give a more complete and comprehensive picture of this period. I have merely tried, to the best of my ability, to record what I personally observed.

But however great the merits of any future stories or accounts, they will all have been written at another period, separated from 1937 by decades; whereas my story was written with the impression of events still fresh in my mind. Herein lies the difference between my story and any others which will be devoted to the years 1937–1938. Herein, I believe, lies its claim to the reader's attention.

It is for this reason that I have not made any changes in it, beyond omitting an introductory passage which today seems irrelevant. Let my *Sofia Petrovna* speak today as a voice from the past, the tale of a witness striving conscientiously, against the powerful forces of falsehood, to discern and record the events which occurred before his eyes.

Moscow, November 1962

1

AFTER the death of her husband, Sofia Petrovna took a course in typing. She felt she simply had to acquire a profession: it would be a long time yet before Kolya began to earn a living. After he got through school he must, whatever happened, take the examination for admission to an institute—Fyodor Ivanovich would never have allowed his son to go without a higher education.

Sofia Petrovna mastered the typewriter easily; but then, she was much more literate than all these modern young ladies. Having received the highest skill rating on her certificate, she soon found herself a job in one of the big Leningrad publishing houses.

Working in an office thoroughly captivated Sofia Petrovna. After a month she simply couldn't understand how she'd ever lived without a job. True, it was unpleasant getting up in the cold of the morning by electric light, and it was shivering cold waiting for the streetcar in a crowd of sleepy, scowling people; true, the clatter of the typewriters gave her a headache toward the end of the working day—but for all that, how fascinating, how interesting working turned out to be! As a little girl she had loved going to school and used to weep when they kept her at home with a cold, and now she loved going to the office.

Seeing that she was conscientious and discreet, they soon made her senior typist—in charge of the typing pool so to speak. It was her job to assign the work, count pages and lines, and clip the sheets together—and Sofia Petrovna liked all this much better than doing the typing herself. Whenever there was a knock at the little wooden window, she'd open it and in a brisk and dignified way take the papers. Most of them were accounts, plans, reports, official letters and orders, but now and again there would be a manuscript from some contemporary writer.

"It will be ready in twenty-five minutes," Sofia Petrovna would say, glancing at the big clock, "exactly. No, exactly twenty-five minutes, no sooner." And she'd slam the little window, preventing further argument.

She'd think a moment, then give the work to the typist she felt was most suitable for the particular job—if the director's secretary brought a document, it went to the one who was most quick, most literate and accurate.

In her youth, feeling lonely sometimes on days when Fyodor Ivanovich was away for a long time visiting patients, she had dreamed of having her own dressmaking shop. In a large, light room pretty girls would sit bent over billowing lengths of silk and she would show them the fashions and engage in worldly conversation with elegant ladies when they came in for fittings.

But the typing pool was even better, more important somehow. Now Sofia Petrovna was often the first person to read a new work of Soviet literature, some story or novel, while it was still only in manuscript form; and although Soviet stories and novels seemed boring to her—there was such a lot about battles and tractors and factory shops and hardly anything about love—she couldn't help being flattered.

She began to curl her hair, which had turned gray early, and when washing it she added a little blueing to the water to keep it from yellowing. In her simple black work smock—relieved by a little collar of genuine old handmade lace—with a carefully sharpened pencil sticking out of the breast pocket, she felt she looked elegant as well as businesslike and efficient.

The typists were a bit afraid of her and called her the schoolmarm behind her back. But they obeyed her. And she wanted to be strict, but fair. In the lunch hour she chatted in a friendly way with those who did their work well and conscientiously, talked about how difficult it was to make out the director's handwriting and how lipstick was far from suitable for everyone. But with those who were capable of typing things like "rehersal" or "collictive" she adopted a haughty manner.

One of the young ladies, Erna Semyonovna, really got on Sofia Petrovna's nerves: she made a mistake in almost every word, smoked in an insolent manner and chattered all the time she was working. Erna Semyonovna vaguely reminded Sofia Petrovna of a fresh housemaid they had once employed in the old days. The maid's name was Fanny, and she'd been rude to Sofia Petrovna and flirted with Fyodor Ivanovich . . . what was the point of holding on to anyone like that!

Of all the typists in the pool, the one Sofia Petrovna liked best was Natasha Frolenko, a modest, rather homely girl with a gray-green complexion. She never made any mistakes in her typing, and her margins and paragraphs were astonishingly elegant. Looking at her work, it would seem she had written on some special paper and used a typewriter better than the other type-writers. But in fact both the paper and the typewriter Natasha used were absolutely the same as all the others, and the whole secret—just think of it—lay in her accuracy.

The typing pool was separated from the rest of the establishment by a door with a little brown-varnished wooden window in it. The door was always kept locked, and all conversations were carried on through the window. At first Sofia Petrovna knew no one at the publishing house except her own typists and the messenger woman who carried the documents. But gradually she got to know everyone.

By the time some two weeks had passed a sedate, bald, but young-looking accountant was coming up to chat with her in the corridor. It turned out he had recognized Sofia Petrovna—some time twenty years earlier Fyodor Ivanovich had treated him very successfully. The accountant was fond of boating and Western European dancing—and Sofia Petrovna was pleased that he suggested that she join their dance club.

The director's secretary, a polite, elderly lady, began to say good morning to her, the head of personnel bowed to her, and so did a well-known writer, a handsome, gray-haired man who wore a beaver fur hat, carried a monogrammed briefcase, and always arrived at the publishing house in his own car. The writer even asked her one day how she liked the last chapter of his novel. "We literary people noticed long ago that typists are the fairest judges. Truly," he said with a smile that showed his even set of false teeth, "they judge a thing spontaneously, they are not guided by preconceived ideas like the comrade critics and editors . . . "

Sofia Petrovna also became acquainted with the party secretary Timofeyev, a lame, unshaven man. He was sullen, looking down at the floor when he spoke, and Sofia Petrovna was a little afraid of him. Occasionally he would appear at the window and ask for Erna Semyonovna—the assistant manager would come with him; Sofia Petrovna would open the door and the assistant manager would drag Erna Semyonovna's typewriter out of the typing pool into the restricted special department. Erna Semyonovna would follow her typewriter with a triumphant expression: as they'd explained to Sofia Petrovna, she had a "security clearance" and the party secretary summoned her to the special department to type up secret party documents.

Soon Sofia Petrovna knew everyone in the publishing house—by name, by position, and by face—ledger clerks, editors, technical editors, messengers. At the end of the first month at the office she saw the director for the first time. The director's office had a thick carpet on the floor, around the table were deep, soft armchairs, and on the table, three whole telephones. The director turned out to be a young man, about thirty-five, no older, a nice height, nicely shaven, wearing a nice gray suit, with three badges on his chest and a fountain pen in his hand. He spoke with Sofia Petrovna for some two minutes, but in those two minutes the telephone rang three times and as he spoke into one, he lifted the receiver off another. The director himself pushed up a chair for her and asked politely whether she would be so kind as to stay late that evening to do some overtime work. She could choose any typist she liked and dictate a report to her. "I am told that you are very good at making out my atrocious writing," he said with a smile.

Sofia Petrovna left his office with a feeling of pride in his authority and flattered by his confidence in her. A well-mannered young man. They said that he was an ordinary worker who'd made his way up—and indeed, his hands looked rough—but apart from that . . .

The first general meeting of the workers of the publishing house which Sofia Petrovna happened to attend seemed boring to her. The director made a short speech about the rise to power of the German fascists and the burning of the reichstag in Germany and then drove away in his Ford. After him the party secretary, Comrade Timofeyev, gave a speech. He paused so long between two sentences that it seemed he'd finished. "We must cor-rob-ber-ate the facts," he said. He was followed by the chairman of the Mestkom,* a stout lady wearing a cameo on her bosom. Wringing and cracking her long fingers, she announced that, in view of all the events, it was first of all essential to tighten up on working hours and wage a relentless war on tardiness. In conclusion, she made a short statement in a hysterical voice about Thaelmann,** and proposed that all workers should join the MOPR.† Sofia Petrovna didn't really understand what it was all about, she was bored and wanted to leave, but she was afraid it wasn't the thing to do and glared at one of the typists who was making her way to the door.

However, soon even these meetings ceased to bore Sofia Petrovna. At one of them, the director, reporting on the fulfillment of the plan, said that the high output figures which had to be achieved depended on conscientious, disciplined work from every member of the collective—not only on the conscientiousness of editors and authors, but also of the cleaning woman and the messenger, and of each individual typist.

"As a matter of fact," he said, "I would like to say that the work of the typing office, under the supervision of Comrade Lipatova, has already attained an exceptionally high standard."

Sofia Petrovna blushed and it was a long time before she dared to raise her eyes again. When she at last decided to look around, she thought everyone seemed extraordinarily kind and attractive, and she found the statistics unexpectedly interesting.

---

*Local trade union committee. (Translator)
**Ernst Thaelmann, German Communist leader. (Translator)
†International Aid to Revolutionaries Organization. (Translator)

2

ALL her free time Sofia Petrovna now spent with Natasha Frolenko. But she had less and less free time. Overtime work or, more often, meetings of the Mestkom, of which Sofia Petrovna soon was a made a member, now took up nearly all her evenings.

Kolya more and more often had to heat up his own dinner and teasingly began to call Sofia Petrovna "mama, the social activist." The Mestkom gave her the job of collecting the union dues. Sofia Petrovna thought very little about why the trade union actually existed, but she liked drawing lines on sheets of paper with a ruler and marking in the various columns who had paid their dues for the current month and who had not; she liked pasting in the stamps and presenting impeccable accounts to the auditing commission. She liked being able to walk into the director's imposing office whenever she chose and remind him jokingly that he was four months in arrears, and have him jokingly present his apologies to his patient comrades on the Mestkom and pull out his wallet and pay up. Even the sullen party secretary could safely be reminded that he owed his dues.

At the end of her first year on the job an important event occurred in Sofia Petrovna's life. She addressed a general meeting of workers on behalf of all the nonparty employees of the publishing house. It happened like this. The publishing house was expecting the arrival of some important comrades from Moscow. The assistant manager, a dashing fellow with meticulously parted hair, ran around the publishing house for days, dragging some kind of frames on his back, and at the most inconvenient moment possible he sent floor polishers into the typing pool office. In the middle of all this, the sullen party secretary came up to Sofia Petrovna in the corridor. "The party organization in conjunction with the Mestkom," he said, looking down at the floor as usual, "has chosen you to give the pledge on behalf of the nonparty activists."

Right before the arrival of the visitors from Moscow there was a mass of work to do. The pool was kept busy typing all sorts of accounts and plans. Practically every evening Sofia Petrovna and Natasha stayed late to do overtime work. The clatter of the typewriters echoed in the empty room. The corridors and offices all around were dark.

Sofia Petrovna liked these evenings. When their work was done, she and Natasha would talk for ages, sitting at their typewriters, before going out into the darkness of the corridor. Natasha didn't say much, but she was a wonderful listener. "Have you noticed that Anna Grigorievna" (the chairman of the Mestkom) "always has dirty nails?" Sofia Petrovna would ask. "And yet she wears a cameo, and waves her hair. She'd do better to wash her hands more often . . . Erna Semyonovna gets on my nerves terribly. She's so insolent . . . And have you noticed, Natasha, that Anna Grigorievna always speaks of the party secretary in a kind of ironical way? She doesn't like him . . ."

After talking about the chairman of the Mestkom and the party secretary, Sofia Petrovna told Natasha about her romance with Fyodor Ivanovich and how Kolya had fallen under the washtub when he was six months old. And what a pretty little boy he'd been, everyone in the street would turn around to look at him. They'd dressed him all in white, a white cape and a white hood.

Natasha somehow seemed to have nothing to tell—not a single romance. "Of course, with a complexion like that . . . " Sofia Petrovna thought to herself. Natasha's life had been nothing but troubles. Her father, a colonel, had died in 1917 of a heart attack. Natasha had been barely five at the time. Their house had been taken away from them, and they had to move in with some relative who was paralyzed. Her mother was a spoiled, helpless woman, they had suffered badly from hunger, and Natasha had gone to work when she was no more than fifteen. Now Natasha was entirely alone; her mother had died the year before last of tuberculosis, her relative had died of old age. Natasha was sympathetic to the Soviet regime, but when she'd applied for Komsomol membership, she'd been turned down.

"My father was a colonel and a homeowner and, you see, they don't believe that I can be truly sympathetic to the regime," said Natasha with a frown. "And perhaps, from the Marxist point of view, they're right . . ."

Her eyes grew red whenever she talked about being refused by the Komsomol, and Sofia Petrovna would quickly change the subject.

The big day arrived. The portraits of Lenin and Stalin had been put into the new frames brought by the assistant manager with his own hands, the director's desk had been covered with red cloth. The Moscow guests—two stout men in foreign-made suits, with foreign-made ties and foreign-made fountain pens in their breast pockets—sat next to the director at the table under the portraits and pulled papers out of their bulging foreign-made briefcases. Next to them the party secretary, in his Russian shirt and jacket, looked very insignificant. The dashing assistant manager and the elevator woman, Marya Ivanovna, bustled around carrying trays of tea, sandwiches, and fruit, offering them to the guests and the director, and then to everyone else.

Sofia Petrovna was so nervous she couldn't listen to the speeches. As though in a trance, she kept her eyes fixed on the water shimmering in the decanter. At a word from the chairman, she went up to the table, turned first toward the director and his guests and then to the meeting, and finally stood facing sideways, hands clasped at her waist as she had been taught to do as a child when reciting greetings in French verse.

"On behalf of the nonparty workers—" she began in a trembling voice, and then went on with the whole pledge to increase labor productivity, everything she and Natasha had composed together and which she had learned by heart.

When she returned home, she didn't go to bed for a long time, but waited for Kolya so she could tell him about the meeting. Kolya was taking his final school examinations and spent every evening at his best friend Alik Finkelstein's; they were studying together.

Sofia Petrovna tidied up the room a little and then went into the kitchen to light the primus stove. "What a pity you don't have a job," she said goodheartedly to the wife of the policeman, who was washing dishes. "It gives you so much to think about, adds so much to your life. Especially if your job is connected with literature."

At last Kolya arrived, hungry and soaked through by the first spring rain, and Sofia Petrovna set before him a plate of cabbage soup. Leaning on her elbows across the table from Kolya watching him eat, she was just about to tell him about her meeting when—

"You know, mother," he said, "I'm now a Komsomol member, the bureau approved my application today."

Having made this announcement, he went on without a breath to something else, stuffing his mouth full of bread—there had been a row at school. "Sashka Yartsev's a real old-regime jerk!"

"Kolya, I don't like it when you use bad language," interrupted Sofia Petrovna.

"But that's not the point: Sashka Yartsev called Alik Finkelstein a Yid. We decided today at the cell meeting to hold a comrades' court show-trial. And you know who's been appointed public prosecutor? Me!"

After he finished eating, Kolya immediately went to bed, and Sofia Petrovna also lay down behind her screen, and in the darkness Kolya recited Mayakovsky to her by heart.

"Now that's real genius, Mama, isn't it?"

And when he had finished, Sofia Petrovna told him about the meeting.

"You're just terrific, Mama," said Kolya and promptly fell asleep.

3

KOLYA finished school, the sweltering summer came, yet Sofia Petrovna still hadn't been given a vacation. They finally gave her time at the end of July. She didn't plan to go anywhere, but all July she dreamed how she'd sleep late in the morning and at last give the apartment the thorough cleaning she'd not had time for since she began her job. She dreamed of taking a break from the staccato drumming of typewriters, of finding Kolya an overcoat, of finally making a visit to the cemetery, and of arranging with a painter to repaint the door.

But when her vacation did finally begin, it turned out relaxing was enjoyable only the first day. Accustomed to a workday schedule, Sofia Petrovna never slept later than eight o'clock; it took the painter just half an hour to repaint the door; Fyodor Ivanovich's grave was entirely in order; she bought a coat for Kolya right away; she darned all the socks in two evenings. The long, empty days dragged, marked by the ticking of the clock, conversations in the kitchen and waiting for Kolya to come home for dinner.

Kolya would disappear for days in the library: he and Alik were preparing to enter college, the mechanical engineering institute, and Sofia Petrovna hardly ever saw him. Very occasionally Natasha Frolenko would drop by, looking tired (she was substituting for Sofia Petrovna at the office), and Sofia Petrovna would eagerly question her about the director's secretary, about the Mestkom chairman's quarrel with the party secretary, and about Erna Semyonovna's spelling mistakes. Also about the discussion in the director's office about the story of that nice writer. The whole editorial department had gathered . . . "Could anyone possibly dislike it?'' exclaimed Sofia Petrovna, clasping her hands. "It describes first love so beautifully. Just like Fyodor Ivanovich and me.''

Sofia Petrovna now completely agreed with Kolya when he expounded to her on the necessity for women to do socially useful work. Yes, everything Kolya said, and everything that was written in the newspapers now seemed to her completely obvious, as if people had always written and talked that way. The one thing Sofia Petrovna really regretted, now that Kolya was grown up, was their former apartment. Other people had been moved in a long time ago during the famine years at the very beginning of the revolution. The family of a policeman named Degtyarenko was moved into Fyodor Ivanovich's former study, the family of an accountant, into the dining room, and Sofia Petrovna and Kolya were left with Kolya's old nursery. Now Kolya was grown, he really needed his own room, after all he wasn't a child any longer.

"But, Mama, would it really be fair for Degtyarenko and his children to live in a basement? Would it!'' asked Kolya severely, explaining to Sofia Petrovna the revolutionary idea behind filling bourgeois apartments with extra tenants. And Sofia Petrovna was obliged to agree with him: it really wasn't quite fair. It was just too bad that Degtyarenko's wife was such a sloven: even in the corridor you could smell the sour odor of her room. She was scared to death of opening the vent window even a crack. And though her twins were already in their sixteenth year, they still made spelling mistakes.

Sofia Petrovna had one consolation for the loss of her apartment: the tenants unanimously elected her official apartment representative. She became, as it were, the manager, the boss of her own apartment. She gently, but firmly, spoke to the wife of the accountant about the trunks standing in the corridor. She calculated the amount each person owed for electricity as accurately as she collected the Mestkom dues at work. She regularly attended the meetings for apartment representatives at the dwelling and rent cooperative association, and then gave a detailed account of what the house manager had said to the other tenants.

On the whole she was on good terms with the other people who lived in the apartment. If Degtyarenko's wife was making jam, she always asked Sofia Petrovna to come into the kitchen and taste whether or not she'd added enough sugar. She'd often drop into Sofia Petrovna's apartment to consult with Kolya as to what she could do to see that the twins, God forbid, did not have to stay back a second year at school. And to gossip with Sofia Petrovna about the accountant's wife, who was a nurse.

"Fall into the hands of that kind of nurse, and you'll soon find yourself in the next world!" Degtyarenko's wife would say.

The accountant himself was a middle-aged man with flabby cheeks and blue veins showing through on his hands and his nose. He was bullied by his wife and daughter, and you never heard him in the apartment. The accountant's red-headed daughter Valya, on the other hand, shocked Sofia Petrovna with phrases like "I'll give her what for!" and "I don't give a damn!" and the accountant's wife, Valya's mother, was truly a nasty woman. Standing over her primus stove with a stony expression, she would relentlessly nag at the policeman's wife about her smoky oil stove or at the timid twins because they hadn't latched the door properly.

She came from the gentry, sprayed the corridor with eau de cologne from an atomizer, wore charms on a chain, and spoke in a quiet voice, barely moving her lips, but the words she used were surprisingly coarse. On paydays Valya would begin to beg her mother for money to buy new shoes.

"Don't even think about it, you horse," her mother would say evenly, and Sofia Petrovna would quickly take refuge in the bathroom so she wouldn't have to hear any more. But soon Valya would come running there herself, to wash her puffy, tearstained face and shout into the sink all the insults she didn't dare say directly to her mother's face.

But in general, apartment No. 46 was a pleasant, peaceful apartment—not like No. 52 above it, where real mayhem occurred almost every week on payday. Degtyarenko, sleepy after coming off duty, would be summoned there regularly, along with the janitor and the house manager, to write up a report.

The vacation dragged on and on—between her room and the kitchen—then finally ended, much to Sofia Petrovna's delight. The rains began, the Summer Garden was strewn with yellow leaves trodden into the mud—and Sofia Petrovna, in galoshes and carrying an umbrella, once again went to the office every day, waited for the streetcar in the morning, and exactly at ten o'clock hung up her number card on the attendance board. Once again she was surrounded by the clack and clatter of typewriters, the rustle of paper and the click of the little door, as it opened and closed: with dignity Sofia Petrovna handed the director's elderly secretary the carefully sorted pages, clipped together and smelling of carbon paper. She pasted the stamps into the trade union membership books, sat in on Mestkom meetings to deal with strengthening worker discipline and the case of a typist who had behaved impolitely to one of the messenger women. As before she was a little afraid of the sullen party secretary, Comrade Timofeyev, and as before did not like the chairman of the Mestkom with the dirty fingernails, she secretly adored the director and envied his secretary—but now they were all familiar to her, and she felt herself at home, sure of herself, and did not hesitate to reproach insolent Erna Semyonovna. Why was she kept on? The question ought to be raised with the Mestkom.

Kolya and Alik passed the exams for the mechanical engineering institute. When they found their names on the list of those who had been accepted, they decided to celebrate by building a radio receiver in the room. Sofia Petrovna didn't like it when Kolya and Alik embarked on some technical project in her room, but she sincerely hoped a radio would prove less expensive than an ice boat. After graduation from high school, Kolya had come up with the idea of building an iceboat so that when winter came they could sail in their own iceboat on the Gulf of Finland. He got hold of some brochure about iceboats and procured some logs, which he and Alik brought up to the room—as a result, it immediately became impossible not only to sweep the floor, but even to move around the room. The logs crowded the dining table over to the wall and the sofa over to the window; they lay in a great triangle on the floor and Sofia Petrovna tripped over them a hundred times a day. But all her entreaties were in vain. In vain she explained to Kolya and Alik that she couldn't have been more uncomfortable had they brought home an elephant. They went on planning and measuring and sketching and sawing until it became perfectly clear that the author of the brochure was an ignoramus, and no iceboat could ever be constructed from his plans.

At that point they sawed up all the logs and meekly burned them in the stove along with the brochure. Sofia Petrovna put everything back in its place and for a whole week couldn't get over the space and cleanliness of her apartment.

At first the radio also brought Sofia Petrovna nothing but distress. Kolya and Alik filled the apartment with wires, screws, bolts and bits of board; they were up until two every morning discussing the relative merits of the different sorts of receivers: then they built their receiver, but wouldn't let Sofia Petrovna listen to anything through to the end as they always wanted to see if they could pick up something else, Norway perhaps, or England; then a passion for perfection overtook them and every evening they took the receiver apart and rebuilt it. Finally, Sofia Petrovna took matters into her own hands, and the radio turned out to be, in fact, a very pleasant invention. She learned how to turn it on and off herself, forbid Kolya and Alik to touch it, and in the evenings would listen to the opera *Faust* or to a concert from Philharmonic Hall.

Natasha Frolenko would also come over to listen. She would bring her embroidery and sit at the table working. She was very good with her hands, she knitted beautifully, sewed, and embroidered napkins and collars. Her whole room was hung with things she'd embroidered, and she set about embroidering a tablecloth for Sofia Petrovna.

On her day off Sofia Petrovna would turn on the radio first thing in the morning: she liked the important, confident voice that announced that Perfume Store No. 4 had received a large consignment of perfumes and eau de cologne, or that a new operetta was to premiere in a few days. She couldn't resist writing down all the telephone numbers they gave just in case. The one thing which did not interest her at all was the latest news on the international situation. Kolya carefully explained to her about the Fascists, about Mussolini, about Chiang Kai-Shek, and she would listen, but only to be polite. When she sat down on the sofa to read the newspaper, she read only the local news and the little satirical column "In the Courts," the editorials and news dispatches would put her to sleep, and the newspaper would fall on her face. What she much preferred to the newspaper were the foreign novels in translation which Natasha brought her from the library like *The Green Hat* or *Hearts of Three*.

The Eighth of March* 1934 was a happy day for Sofia Petrovna. In the morning the messenger woman from the publishing house brought her a basket of flowers. There was a card in the basket which read, "To the nonparty worker, Sofia Petrovna Lipatova, congratulations on the Eighth of March. From the Party Organization and the Mestkom." She put the flowers on Kolya's desk, under the shelf which held the collected works of Lenin, next to the little bust of Stalin. She felt happy all day. She decided she wouldn't throw out the flowers when they wilted, but would dry them and put them away in a book as a keepsake.

---

*Women's Day, an official holiday in the Soviet Union. (Translator)

4

Sofia Petrovna was in her third year at the office. They had given her a raise, she now received not two hundred and fifty rubles, but three hundred and seventy-five. Kolya and Alik were still studying, but they were already earning quite a bit doing drafting at some design office. For Sofia Petrovna's birthday Kolya bought her a small tea service with his own money: a creamer, a teapot, a sugar bowl, and three cups. Sofia Petrovna didn't much like the pattern on the china—some sort of red squares on a yellow background. She would have preferred flowers. But the porcelain was fine and of good quality, and what did it really matter? It was a present from her son.

Her son had become handsome, with his gray eyes and black brows, tall, and more confident, calm, and cheerful than Fyodor Ivanovich had been even in his best years. He had a sort of military way about him always, tidy and energetic. Sofia Petrovna would look at him with both tenderness and fear, glad and yet afraid to be glad. What a good-looking young man, and healthy, too, he didn't drink or smoke, a good son and loyal Komsomol member. Of course Alik was a polite, hard-working young man also, but nothing compared to Kolya! His father was a bookbinder in Vinnitsa, with masses of children, very poor. Alik since early childhood had lived in Leningrad with an aunt, and it was clear that she didn't take very good care of him: his clothes were patched at the elbows, his shoes were shabby, and he himself was short and puny. And his brain wasn't as good as Kolya's either.

One thought constantly bothered Sofia Petrovna: Kolya was already over twenty, and he still didn't have his own room.

Wasn't her constant presence keeping him from leading his own life? Kolya apparently had fallen in love with someone at the institute: she had questioned Alik about it, discreetly—who was she? what was her name? how old was she? was she a good student? who were her parents? But Alik answered evasively, and the look in his eyes made it clear he was not going to give the secret away. All Sofia Petrovna could get out of him was the girl's name: Nata. But it didn't matter what her name was or whether the love was really serious or merely infatuation—the fact remained that it was absolutely essential that a young man of his age have his own room.

Sofia Petrovna shared her anxious thoughts with Natasha. Natasha listened without saying anything, then blushed and said that yes . . . without question . . . it would be better if Nikolai Fyodorovich had his own room . . . but, well . . . she, for instance, lived alone . . . without her mother . . . and so? . . . oh, nothing!

Natasha broke off and fell silent and Sofia Petrovna never did understand what exactly it was that she was trying to say.

Sofia Petrovna considered all possible ways to exchange her one room for two and even began to set aside money in a savings bank so as to be able to pay more, if necessary. But the question of a separate room for Kolya unexpectedly lost its urgency: the honor students Nikolai Fyodorovich Lipatov and Aleksander Finkelstein, according to some kind of labor allotment, were to be sent as experts to Uralmash (Ural Engineering Works) in Sverdlovsk. They were short of engineering and technical workers there. The institute made arrangements for them to finish their studies by correspondence.

"Don't worry, Mama," said Kolya, placing his great big hand over Sofia Petrovna's small one. "Don't worry, Alik and I will manage just fine there . . . They have promised us a room in a dormitory . . . And Sverdlovsk isn't far away, after all. You'll be able to come see us some time . . . and . . . you know what? You can send us parcels."

Every day after that, as soon as she got home from work, Sofia Petrovna set about sorting Kolya's clothes in the dresser, sewing, darning, and ironing. She took Fyodor Ivanovich's old suitcase to be repaired. Today that spring morning when she and Fyodor

Ivanovich had gone together to buy the suitcase at the Guard Regiment's store seemed infinitely long ago, like some unreal morning in some unreal life. She glanced curiously at the page from *Niva* which had been glued over a tear in the side: a picture of a lady in a low-cut gown with a long train and her hair piled on top of her head amazed her. To think that fashions were really like that in those days.

Kolya's departure worried Sofia Petrovna and made her sad, but she couldn't help admiring the skill and care with which he packed his books and the large notebooks filled with his clear handwriting, and himself sewed his Komsomol membership card into the waist of his trousers. For a long time the day of his departure was a week away, then suddenly it was tomorrow.

"Kolya, are you ready, Kolya?" asked Alik Finkelstein, coming into the room that morning, so little, but with such a big head and protruding ears. "What about it?"

A new jacket wrinkled across his back, the ends of his shirt collar turned down. Kolya strode over to his suitcase and picked it up as easily as if it had been empty. He virtually swung his suitcase all the way to the station, while poor Alik, puffing and wiping the sweat from his forehead with his sleeve, could barely drag his small trunk. With his short legs and big head, he reminded Sofia Petrovna of some comic character from a cartoon film. Alik's aunt, needless to say, did not bother to come to the station to see him off, so the three of them—Kolya, Sofia Petrovna, and Alik—strolled staidly up and down the platform in the damp gloom of the station.

Kolya and Alik were having a heated discussion on the question: which was the lighter and more durable automobile, the Fiat or the Packard? And it was not until five minutes before the train was scheduled to leave that Sofia Petrovna remembered she hadn't told the boys to be careful about thieves on the trip or about their laundry. They must never give their clothing to the laundress without first counting it and making a list . . . And under no circumstances should they eat vinaigrette salad in a canteen—it was often left over from the day before, and it was so easy to catch typhoid fever.

She took Alik aside and clutched him by the shoulder. "Alik, my dear," she said, "please, my dear, look after Kolya."

Alik looked at her through his glasses with his big, kind eyes. "Is that so difficult? Certainly I'll keep an eye on Kolya. Don't you worry."

It was time to get on the train. A moment later Kolya and Alik appeared at the window, Kolya tall, Alik up to his shoulder. Kolya said something to Sofia Petrovna, but it couldn't be heard through the window. He laughed, took off his cap and looked around the compartment, excited and happy. Alik was forming letters for Sofia Petrovna with his fingers: "Don't" . . . she made out and waved at him, guessing he wanted to say "don't worry" . . . My God, they're just children and off on such a journey!

A moment later she was walking back along the platform, alone in the crowd of people, walking faster and faster, not noticing where she was going, wiping her eyes with her fingers.

5

A FTER Kolya's departure Sofia Petrovna spent even less time at home. There was always enough overtime work at the office, and she stayed late nearly every evening, saving up money to buy Kolya a suit: a young engineer had to dress decently.

On her free evenings she took Natasha home with her for tea. They would stop together at the food store on the corner and choose two pastries. Sofia Petrovna would make tea in the teapot with the squares on it and turn on the radio. Natasha brought her embroidery. Recently, on Sofia Petrovna's advice, she had been taking brewer's yeast regularly, but her color did not improve.

On one such evening, just as she was leaving Sofia Petrovna's to go home, Natasha suddenly asked her to give her Kolya's latest photo. "The only photo I've got in my room now is one of my mother," she explained.

Sofia Petrovna gave her the photo of Kolya, handsome and big-eyed, in a collar and tie. The photographer had caught his smile perfectly.

One day, on the way back from work, they went to a movie— and from then on the movies became their favorite pastime. They both loved films about airmen and border guards. The pilots with their white teeth, accomplishing great feats, reminded her of Kolya. She liked the new songs resounding from the screen— particularly "Thank you, my heart!" and "When my Country Calls, I'll be a Hero;" she liked the word "Motherland." This word, written with a capital letter, gave her a warm, proud feeling. And when the best pilot or the bravest border guard fell backwards, struck by an enemy bullet, Sofia Petrovna would clutch Natasha's hand, just as she had clutched Fyodor Ivanovich's hand in her youth when the movie star Vera Kholodnaya would suddenly pull a small woman's revolver from a wide muff and, raising it slowly, take aim at the forehead of the villain.

Natasha again applied for admission to the Komsomol, and again was turned down. Sofia Petrovna sympathized deeply with Natasha's grief; the poor girl was so in need of company! And why, exactly, didn't they take her? The girl was a hard worker and absolutely loyal to the Soviet regime. For one thing, she worked better than any of them. For another, she was politically aware. She wasn't like Sofia Petrovna, she didn't let a day go by without reading *Pravda* from beginning to end. Natasha understood everything as well as Kolya and Alik did, from the international situation to the construction projects of the five-year plan.

And how she worried when the *Chelushkin* was crushed by the ice; she remained glued to the radio. She cut out of every newspaper the photographs of Captain Voronin, Schmidt's camp and then the pilots. When the news of the first rescues were announced, she wept at her typewriter, tears of happiness fell on her paper, and she spoiled two pages. "They won't let people perish, no they won't," she repeated, wiping her eyes. Such a sincere, warmhearted girl! And once again they had turned her down for the Komsomol. It was unfair.

Sofia Petrovna even wrote to Kolya about the injustice Natasha had suffered. But Kolya replied that injustice was a class concept and vigilance was essential. Natasha did after all come from a bourgeois, landowning family. Vile fascist hirelings, of the kind that had murdered comrade Kirov, had still not been entirely eradicated from the country. The class struggle was still going on, and therefore it was essential to exercise the utmost vigilance when admitting people to the Party and the Komsomol. He also wrote that in a few years they would undoubtedly admit Natasha, and strongly advised her to take notes on the work of Lenin, Stalin, Marx and Engels.

"In a few years . . ." Natasha smiled bitterly. "Nikolai Fyodorovich forgets that I'll soon be twenty-four."

"Then you'll be admitted straight into the party," Sofia Petrovna said consolingly. "And what's twenty-four! First youth."

Natasha said nothing in return, but when she left that evening she borrowed from Sofia Petrovna a volume of Kolya's Lenin.

Kolya's letters arrived regularly once a week, on Saturdays. What a wonderful son he was—never forgot that his mother worried about him, though he certainly had plenty to do there! When she returned from work, she would start getting her key out of her bag while she was still at the bottom of the stairs, rush up, and when she finally reached the fourth floor, out of breath, she would open the blue mailbox. The letter in the yellow envelope was already waiting for her. Without taking off her coat, she would sit down near the window and spread out the carefully folded sheets of notebook paper.

"Hello, Mama!" every letter began. "I hope that you are well. I'm fine. Production at our factory in the last week reached . . ."

The letters were long, but they were mostly about the factory, about the growth of the Stakhanovite* movement; about himself, about his own life—not a word.

"Just think," Kolya wrote in his first letter, "all the worm gears, milling cutters, even the broaches, everything we have is still foreign-made, we pay gold to the capitalists for everything, and somehow can't make them ourselves."

But Sofia Petrovna wasn't interested in milling cutters. What she wanted to know was what he and Alik were getting to eat, was the laundress there honest? did they have enough money? and when did they find time to study? at night, or when? Kolya answered all these questions in a very cursory and incomprehensible way. Sofia Petrovna so wanted to be able to imagine what their room was like, how they lived, and what they ate that, on Natasha's advice, she wrote a letter to Alik.

The answer came a few days later. "Dear Sofia Petrovna!" wrote Alik. "Forgive me for being blunt, but you have no reason to worry about Nikolai's health. We eat quite well. I buy sausage in the evening and fry it myself in butter in the morning. We eat lunch in the canteen, three courses, not bad at all. The jam which you sent us we decided to have only with our evening tea, and

---

*A movement urging workers to ever-greater efforts, named for Alexei Stakhanov, a coal miner who purportedly exceeded production norms. (Translator)

this way it will last us a long time. I also look after the laundry and count it. We have set aside certain hours every day for our studies. You may be absolutely assured that I do everything I can for Nikolai, as his friend and comrade, and will try to continue to do so.''

The letter concluded: "Nikolai is successfully developing a method for the production of Fellows' cogwheel cutters in our machine-tool workshop. In the factory party committee they say he's the rising eagle of the future.''

Of course, it's the sun that rises, not eagles, and Sofia Petrovna certainly had no idea what a Fellows' cogwheel cutter was— but still these words filled her heart with pride and delight.

Sofia Petrovna put Kolya's letters carefully away in a box which had once held writing paper. There, too, she kept the letters Fyodor Ivanovich had written her when they were engaged, photographs of Kolya when he was little, and a photograph of the infant Karina, who had been born aboard the *Chelushkin*. Sofia Petrovna put Alik's letter there also: he undoubtedly was loyal to Kolya and understood him very well!

One day, about ten months after Kolya's departure, Sofia Petrovna received through the mail an impressive-looking plywood crate. From Sverdlovsk. From Kolya. The crate was so heavy the mailman had a hard time bringing it up to the room and demanded a ruble as a tip. "A sewing machine, perhaps?'' thought Sofia Petrovna. "That would be nice!'' She had sold hers when times were hard.

The postman left, and Sofia Petrovna took a hammer and a knife and opened the box. Inside lay a mysterious black steel object. It was carefully packed in wood shavings. Not exactly a wheel, not exactly a bore, God knows what it was. Then at last, on the black back of the unknown object, Sofia Petrovna discovered a label on which was written, in Kolya's handwriting: "Dear Mama, I'm sending you the first cogwheel cut with the Fellows' cogwheel cutter produced at our factory by my method.''

Sofia Petrovna laughed, patted the cogwheel, and puffing, hoisted it onto the window sill. Every time she looked at it, she felt cheerful.

A few days later, when Sofia Petrovna was drinking her morning tea, in a hurry to get to work, Natasha unexpectedly burst into her room. Her hair was disheveled and wet with snow, one of her boots was unfastened. She handed Sofia Petrovna a wet newspaper.

"Look . . . I just bought it on the corner . . . I start reading . . . and all of a sudden I see Nikolai Fyodorovich. Kolya."

On the first page of *Pravda* Sofia Petrovna saw Kolya's smiling face. The photograph made him look different, a little older, but without a doubt it was he, her son, Kolya. Under the portrait was a caption:

> Industrial enthusiast, Komsomol member Nikolai Lipatov,
> who has developed a method for the manufacture of Fellows'
> cogwheel cutters at the Ural Machine-building factory.

Natasha hugged Sofia Petrovna and kissed her on the cheek. "Dear Sofia Petrovna!" she entreated, "please, let's send him a telegram."

Sofia Petrovna had never seen Natasha so excited. Her own hands were shaking and she couldn't find her briefcase anywhere. They composed the telegram at the office, during the lunch break, and sent it after work. Everyone congratulated Sofia Petrovna: at the office even Erna Semyonovna congratulated her on having a son like that; at home, even the nurse.

As she went to bed that night, happy and tired, it occurred to Sofia Petrovna for the first time that Natasha was probably in love with Kolya. How could she not have guessed it earlier? A good girl, well brought up, hard-working, only so very homely and older than he.

As she fell asleep, Sofia Petrovna tried to picture to herself the girl Kolya would fall in love with and make his wife: tall, fresh, rosy, with bright eyes and light hair—very like an English postcard, only with a "KIM"* badge on her breast. Nata?: no, better Svetlana. Or Ludmila: Milochka.

---

*Communist Youth International. (Translator)

6

NEW Year 1937 drew near. The Mestkom decided to give a party for the children of the people who worked at the publishing house. Sofia Petrovna was put in charge of organizing the event. She picked Natasha as her assistant, and soon their work was in full swing.

They telephoned the homes of the employees to find out the names and ages of the children; typed out invitations; ran around the shops buying candy, gingerbread, glass balls, and party favors; and wore themselves out looking for artificial snow. The most important and most difficult job was deciding which gift to give to each child so they'd please everybody without going over their budget. Sofia Petrovna and Natasha almost came to quarreling over the present for the director's little girl. Sofia Petrovna wanted to buy her a big doll—bigger than for the other little girls—but Natasha felt that would be indelicate. They compromised on a pretty little trumpet with a fluffy tassel.

Finally the only thing which remained to be bought was the New Year's tree. They bought a tall one, going right up to the ceiling, with thick, full branches. On the day of the party, Natasha, Sofia Petrovna, and Marya Ivanovna, the elevator woman, decorated the tree from early morning until two in the afternoon. Marya Ivanovna entertained them with stories about the director's wife: when she referred to the director himself, she used the pronoun "they" in the old way. The elevator woman handed Natasha and Sofia Petrovna the glass balls and the paper favors, the little mailboxes and silver ships, and Natasha and Sofia Petrovna hung them on the tree.

Before long Sofia Petrovna's legs began to bother her and she seated herself in an armchair and began to place little slips of paper inscribed with ''Thank you, Comrade Stalin, for a happy childhood'' into the packages of candy. Natasha continued decorating the tree by herself. She had magic fingers and wonderfully good taste: the way she put up Grandfather Frost was really very effective. Then Sofia Petrovna glued the curly head of the child Lenin in the center of a big, red, five-pointed star, and Natasha put it up on the very top of the tree—and everything was ready. They took down the full-length portrait of Stalin and replaced it with another—of Stalin sitting with a little girl on his knee. That was the portrait Sofia Petrovna liked best of all.

Three o'clock. Time to go home, rest a little, have dinner and change for the party.

The party was a wonderful success. All the children came and almost all the papas and mamas. The director's wife was not there, but the director came and brought his little daughter himself, an enchanting little girl with blond hair.

The children were delighted with their presents, the parents went into raptures over the tree. Only Anna Grigorievna, the chairman of the Mestkom committee, was offended because her son was given a drum and not wooden soldiers like the son of the party secretary: the soldiers were more expensive. She was wearing a green silk dress, décolleté to boot. Her son, a lanky unpleasant boy, whistled and hit the drum ostentatiously with his fist and broke it. All the others were pleased. The daughter of the director blew on her trumpet all the time, hopping up and down between her father's knees, pushing her chubby hand against his knee and tipping her head back to look at the tree.

Sofia Petrovna felt herself the real mistress of the ball. She wound up the Gramophone, switched on the radio, indicated to the elevator woman with her eyes to whom to offer the plates of candies. She felt sorry for Natasha, who stood timidly next to the wall, pale and gray-looking, in her best blouse which she had embroidered herself. The director, bending down, took his little girl by both hands and warned her that Grandfather Frost would be angry if she did not behave. Sofia Petrovna was touched by this scene: she hoped that Kolya would be just like the director. Who knows, in two years perhaps, she might have just such a sweet little granddaughter. Or a grandson. She would persuade Kolya to call her grandson Vladlen*—a lovely name!—or a granddaughter Ninel—an elegant, French-sounding name, and if you read it backward it became Lenin.

Sofia Petrovna, tired out, sank down into a chair. She was thinking it was time she went home, she was getting a migraine headache, when the impressive-looking accountant approached, and bowing politely, told her a fearful bit of news: a large number of physicians in the city had been arrested. The accountant was personally acquainted with all the leading medical men in town. His eczema resisted everyone's treatments, Fyodor Ivanovich was the only one who had succeeded in getting rid of it. ("There was a real doctor for you! The others sprinkle powders about, smear on ointments, but all to no effect . . .") Among those arrested, the accountant named Doctor Kiparisov, a colleague of Fyodor Ivanovich and Kolya's godfather.

"What? Doctor Kiparisov? . . . It can't be! What happened? Could there really have been another . . . accident?" asked Sofia Petrovna.

The accountant raised his eyes sanctimoniously and went away, walking on tiptoe for some reason.

Two years before, after the murder of Kirov (Oh! what grim times those were! Patrols walked the streets . . . and when Comrade Stalin was about to arrive, the station square was cordoned off by troops . . . and there were troops lining all the streets as Stalin walked behind the coffin)—after Kirov's murder there had also been many arrests, but at that time they first took all kinds of oppositionists, then old regime people, all kinds of "vons" and barons. But now it was doctors.

After the murder of Kirov they had sent away, as a member of the nobility, Madame Nezhentseva, an old friend of Sofia Petrovna's—they had attended school together. Sofia Petrovna had been astonished: what connection could Madame Nezhentseva possibly have to the murder? She taught French in a school and lived just like everybody else. But Kolya had explained that it was necessary to rid Leningrad of unreliable elements. "And

---

*Vladimir Lenin in combined form. Both Vladlen and Ninel were popular names at the time. (Translator)

31

who exactly is this Madame Nezhentseva of yours anyway? You remember yourself, Mama, that she didn't recognize Mayakovsky as a poet and always said that things were cheaper in the old days. She's not a real Soviet person . . ." All right, but what about the doctors? What were they guilty of? Just imagine—Ivan Ignatyich Kiparisov! Such an esteemed doctor!

The children were noisy in the cloakroom. Sofia Petrovna, acting as a hostess, helped the parents find boots and leggings. The director, carrying his daughter in his arms, came up to her to say goodbye. He thanked the Mestkom for the splendid party.

"I saw the portrait of your son in *Pravda*," he told her with a smile. "It's a fine new generation growing up to take our place . . ."

Sofia Petrovna looked at him with adoration. She wanted to say that he had no right yet to talk of being replaced—what was thirty-five after all? The prime of life!—but she didn't dare.

He dressed his little girl himself, wrapping her up in a fluffy white scarf over her little fur coat. How skillfully he did everything. Her mother didn't have to worry about letting him take the child out. A wonderful family man—one could see that at a glance.

7

THE papers said nothing about the doctors or about Dr. Kiparisov. Sofia Petrovna intended to call on Mrs. Kiparisova, but couldn't bring herself to. There was no time, and anyway it was a bit awkward. She hadn't seen Mrs. Kiparisova for about three years. She couldn't very well suddenly go and visit her, out of the blue.

In January articles began to appear in the newspapers about an upcoming new trial. The trial of Kamenev and Zinoviev had made a great impression on Sofia Petrovna, but she was too unused to reading the papers to follow it in detail every day. But this time Natasha got her into reading the papers, and they read all the articles about the trial together every day. There was more and more talk everywhere about fascist spies, and terrorists and arrests . . .

Just think, these scoundrels wanted to murder our beloved Stalin. It was they, it turned out, who had murdered Kirov. They caused explosions in mines and derailed trains. And there was scarcely an establishment in which they hadn't placed their henchmen.

One of the typists in the office, just back from a vacation resort, related that there was a young engineer in the room next to theirs, she sometimes went for walks with him in the park. Then one night a car suddenly drove up and he was arrested: it turned out he was a saboteur. Yet he looked such a decent person—you never could tell.

In Sofia Petrovna's building, too, in apartment 104 opposite hers, someone was arrested—some Communist or other.

His room was closed up with red seals on the door. The house manager told Sofia Petrovna about it.

In the evenings Sofia Petrovna put on her glasses—she had recently become farsighted—and read the paper out loud to Natasha. The tablecloth was already finished; Natasha was now embroidering a coverlet for Sofia Petrovna's bed.

They discussed how indignant Kolya must be just now. And not only Kolya: all decent people were indignant. Why, the trains derailed by the saboteurs might contain children! What heartlessness! Monsters! It was not for nothing the Trotskyites were hand in glove with the Gestapo: they really were no better than the fascists who were murdering children in Spain. And was it really possible that Dr. Kiparisov had been part of their bandit gang? He had often been invited to a consultation along with Fyodor Ivanovich. After the consultation Fyodor Ivanovich would bring him home to have a cup of tea and visit for a while. Sofia Petrovna had seen him close up—just as she could see Natasha now. And now he had joined a gang of bandits! Who would have thought it? Such a worthy old man.

One evening, after reading in the paper about all the crimes committed by the accused and hearing the same thing on the radio, she and Natasha had such a vivid picture of heaps of mutilated bodies with arms and legs torn off that Sofia Petrovna was afraid to spend the night alone and Natasha was afraid to walk home through the streets. That night Natasha spent the night with her, sleeping on the couch.

Everywhere, in every enterprise and every establishment, meetings were held, and their publishing house held one, too, to discuss the trial. The chairman of the Mestkom went around to all the rooms beforehand and warned everyone that in case anyone had so little sense of responsibility as to intend leaving before the meeting, he would do well to bear in mind that the outside door would be locked. Absolutely everyone came to the meeting, even the members of the editorial section, who usually skipped them.

The director made a speech in which he briefly, dryly, and precisely summarized the information which had been in the papers. He was followed by the party secretary, Comrade Timofeyev. Pausing after every few words, he declared the enemies of the people were active everywhere, that they might infiltrate even our establishment and that it was therefore necessary for all honest workers to increase incessantly their political vigilance. The chairman of the Mestkom, Anna Grigorievna, was then given the floor.

"Comrades!" she began, then closed her eyes and fell silent a moment. "Comrades!" She clasped her thin hands with their long nails. "The vile enemy has thrust his dirty paw into our establishment, too."

Everyone froze. The cameo rose and fell on Anna Grigorievna's ample bosom.

"Arrested last night was the ex-supervisor of our print shop, now unmasked as an enemy of the people—Gerasimov. He turned out to be the nephew of the Moscow Gerasimov, who was unmasked a month ago. With the connivance of our party organization, which is suffering, to use Comrade Stalin's apt expression, from the idiotic disease of complacency, Gerasimov continued to, so to speak, 'operate' in our print shop even after his own uncle, the Moscow Gerasimov, had been unmasked."

She sat down. Her bosom rose and fell.

"No questions?" asked the director, who was presiding at the meeting.

"And what did they . . . do . . . in the print shop?" Natasha asked timidly.

The director nodded at the chairman of the Mestkom.

"What did they do?" she repeated in a shrill voice, rising from her chair. "I think, Comrade Frolenko, I just explained in plain Russian that ex-supervisor of our print shop Gerasimov turned out to be the nephew of the Moscow Gerasimov. He maintained daily family contact with his uncle . . . undermined the Stakhanovite movement in the print shop . . . wrecked the plan . . . on the orders of his relative. With the criminal connivance of our party organization."

Natasha asked nothing more.

Returning home after the meeting, Sofia Petrovna sat down to write a letter to Kolya. She wrote him that enemies had been discovered in their print shop. And how were things at Uralmash? Was everything all right? As a loyal Komsomol member, Kolya needed to be vigilant.

At the publishing house there was a distinct feeling of uneasiness. The director was summoned daily to Smolny.* The sullen party secretary was constantly coming into the typing office, opening the door with his own private key, and calling Erna Semyonovna into the special department. The polite accountant, who somehow always seemed to know everything, told Sofia Petrovna that the party organization was now meeting every evening.

"It's a lovers' quarrel," he said with a knowing smile. "Anna Grigorievna is blaming everything on the party secretary, and the party secretary, on the director. As far as I understand, there's to be a change of management."

"The blame for what?" asked Sofia Petrovna.

"Why . . . they simply can't agree which one of them it was who overlooked Gerasimov."

Sofia Petrovna didn't get it at all and left the publishing house that day with a vague sense of alarm. On the street she noticed a tall old woman with a scarf over her hat, wearing felt boots with galoshes over them, and carrying a cane. The old woman walked along using her cane to avoid slippery places. Her face looked familiar to Sofia Petrovna. Why, it was Mrs. Kiparisova! Could it really be she? Good God, how she had changed!

"Maria Erastovna!" Sofia Petrovna called out to her.

Mrs. Kiparisova stopped, raised her large black eyes, and with an obvious effort managed a smile of greeting.

"Hello, Sofia Petrovna! What a long time it's been! Your son must be quite grown up by now?" She stood, holding Sofia Petrovna by the hand, but didn't look her in the eye. Her huge eyes darted about in confusion.

"Maria Erastovna," said Sofia Petrovna warmly. "I'm so glad I met you. I heard that you've had some trouble . . . about Ivan Ignatyich . . . Listen, we're friends after all . . . Ivan Ignatyich was Kolya's godfather . . . that doesn't count any more, of course, but we belong to the older generation, you and I. Tell me, has Ivan Ignatyich been accused of anything serious? Surely there can't be any grounds for such an accusation? I simply just can't believe it. Such a wonderful, highly esteemed doctor! My

---

*Leningrad Party Headquarters. (Translator)

36

husband always had the highest respect for him and looked up to him as a clinical physician."

"Ivan Ignatyich did nothing against the Soviet regime," said Mrs. Kiparisova gloomily.

"I was sure of it!" exclaimed Sofia Petrovna. "I never doubted it a minute, and said so to everyone . . ."

Mrs. Kiparisova looked at her mournfully with her great dark eyes.

"Good-bye, Sofia Petrovna," she said without a smile.

"When Ivan Ignatyich returns, invite me over to celebrate," Sofia Petrovna went on. "And really, why are you so upset? Since Ivan Ignatyich isn't guilty—then everything will be all right. Nothing can happen to an honest man in our country. It's just a misunderstanding. Come on, don't be discouraged . . . Stop by and have a cup of tea sometime!"

Mrs. Kiparisova walked away along the pavement, tapping the ice with her stick.

"Could I have aged that much, too?" thought Sofia Petrovna. "Her face is so dark and wrinkled. No, it's not possible, I'm not like that yet. She's simply let herself go terribly: the felt boots, the cane, the scarf . . . It's very important for a woman not to let herself go, to take care of herself. Who on earth wears felt boots these days? It's not 1918. She looks sixty-five—and she can't be more than fifty. . . . It's good that Kiparisov isn't guilty. Other people are one thing, but a wife knows. I always thought it was just a misunderstanding and nothing else."

8

THE next day the typing office was rushing to finish the semi-annual report. Everyone knew the director was taking the Red Arrow* to Moscow that night to report to the press department of the Party Central Committee on the half year's work of the publishing house. Sofia Petrovna urged the typists to hurry. Natasha worked right through the lunch hour without a break.

By three o'clock the report lay on Sofia Petrovna's desk and she carefully sorted out the four copies. Not begrudging the clips, she clipped the pages evenly together.

Still the director's secretary did not come for the report. Sofia Petrovna decided to take it to the office herself.

She ran into the party secretary outside the half-open door of the director's office. "You can't go in there!" he told her, without even a nod, and limped off into another room. He looked all disheveled.

Sofia Petrovna glanced through the half-open door. An unfamiliar man was kneeling in front of the desk taking papers out of a drawer. The whole carpet was covered with papers.

"What time will Comrade Zakharov be here today?" Sofia Petrovna asked the elderly secretary.

"He's been arrested," the secretary answered voicelessly, moving only her lips, "last night."

Her lips were blue.

Sofia Petrovna took the report back to the office. When she reached the office door, she felt her knees give way beneath her. The sound of the typewriters deafened her. "Do they know

*Express night train to Moscow. (Translator)

39

already or not?'' They clattered on as if nothing had happened. If she'd been told the director had died, she wouldn't have been so stunned. She sat down at her desk and began mechanically taking the clips off the sheets of paper.

Timofeyev came in, opening the door with his own key. Sofia Petrovna noticed for the first time that despite his lameness the party secretary held himself erect and walked with a firm step. ''Excuse me!'' she said in a frightened voice when he brushed her shoulder accidentally in passing.

At four-thirty the bell rang at last. Sofia Petrovna went silently downstairs, silently put on her coat and hat and went out into the street. It was thawing. Sofia Petrovna stopped in front of a puddle, wondering how to get around it. Natasha came up to her. Natasha already knew. Erna Semyonovna had told her.

''Natasha,'' began Sofia Petrovna, when they had reached the corner where they usually parted. ''Natasha, do you believe that Zakharov is guilty of something? No, it's nonsense . . . Natasha, after all we know . . .''

She couldn't find the words to express her certainty. Zakharov, the Bolshevik, their director whom they saw every day, Zakharov, a saboteur! That was an impossibility, nonsense, balderdash, as Fyodor Ivanovich used to say. He was such an eminent party man. They knew him at Smolny, and in Moscow, they couldn't arrest him by mistake. He wasn't some Kiparisov!

Natasha was silent.

''Let's go to your house, I'll explain everything to you,'' said Natasha suddenly with unusual solemnity.

They went in. Silently they took off their coats. Natasha took a carefully folded newspaper out of her old briefcase. She opened the newspaper in front of Sofia Petrovna and pointed out a special article on the center page to Sofia Petrovna.

Sofia Petrovna put on her glasses.

''Understand, my dear, he could have been seduced,'' said Natasha in a whisper, ''a woman . . .''

Sofia Petrovna began to read.

The article recounted the case of a certain Soviet citizen, A., a loyal party member, who was sent by the Soviet government on a mission to Germany to study the use of a new chemical. In Germany, he fulfilled his duties conscientiously, but soon he became involved with a certain S., an elegant young woman who professed to be sympathetic to the Soviet Union. S. paid frequent visits to citizen A. in his apartment. Then one day citizen A. discovered that certain important political documents were missing from his office. The landlady informed him that S. had come to his room when he was not there. Citizen A. had sufficient courage to break off with S. immediately, but not sufficient courage to tell his comrades about the disappearance of the documents. He went back to the U.S.S.R., hoping by his honest work as a Soviet engineer to atone for the crime against his homeland. For a whole year he worked peacefully and was already beginning to forget about his crime. But hidden agents of the Gestapo, infiltrating into our country, began to blackmail him. Terrorized, A. handed over to them secret plans from the factory at which he worked. The valiant Chekists* unmasked the entrenched agents of fascism: the investigation led back to the unfortunate A.

"Do you understand?" Natasha asked in a whisper. "The investigation . . . Our director is, of course, a fine person, a loyal party member. But citizen A., they write here, was also a loyal party member at first . . . Any loyal party member can be ensnared by a pretty woman."

Natasha could not stand pretty women. She recognized only classic beauty and couldn't find it in anyone.

"They say our director has been abroad," Natasha recalled. "Also on a mission. Remember Marya Ivanovna, the elevator woman, told us that he'd brought his wife a light-blue knitted suit from Berlin?"

The article shook Sofia Petrovna's certainty, but she still couldn't believe it. Some citizen A. was one thing, their Zakharov quite another. A staunch party member, he had reported on the trial himself. And under him the publishing house had always overfulfilled its plan.

"But, Natasha, after all we know . . ." said Sofia Petrovna wearily.

"What do we know?" retorted Natasha hotly. "We know he was director of our publishing house, but we don't actually know

---

*Members of the Secret Police. (Translator)

41

anything more than that. Do we really know about his personal life? Can you really vouch for him?"

And in fact, Sofia Petrovna hadn't the slightest idea as to what Comrade Zakharov did when he wasn't presiding at publishing house meetings or leading his little girl up to the New Year's tree. All men, every last one of them, were terribly fond of pretty women. Any cheeky housemaid could wrap any man, even a decent one, around her little finger. If Sofia Petrovna had not thrown Fanny out in time, there's no telling how her flirtation with Fyodor Ivanovich might have ended.

"Let's have some tea," said Sofia Petrovna.

Over tea they remembered there was something military about Zakharov's bearing. Straight back and broad shoulders. Perhaps he'd been a White officer in his time? He was certainly old enough to have been.

They had nothing to eat with their tea. They were both too tired to bother going down to the store for a loaf of bread or some pastries. "It's going to be grim at the office tomorrow," thought Sofia Petrovna. "Like having a corpse in the house. Say what you like, it's sad about the director." She remembered the half-open door of the office and the man on his knees in front of the desk. Only now she understood that a search had been going on.

Natasha got ready to leave. She carefully folded the newspaper and hid it in her briefcase. Then she poured herself a glass of hot water from the kettle and warmed her large red hands on it before going out. Her hands had been frostbitten in childhood, and they were always cold.

Suddenly the doorbell rang. And a second time. Sofia Petrovna went to open it. Two rings, that meant it was for her. Who could have come so late?

Behind the door stood Alik Finkelstein.

To see Alik there alone, without Kolya, was unnatural.

"Kolya!?" Sofia Petrovna cried, grabbing Alik by the dangling end of his scarf. "Typhoid?"

Alik, without looking at her, slowly took off his galoshes.

"Shhh!" he said at last. "Let's go into your room."

And he tiptoed along the corridor, in a bowlegged, comical way.

Sofia Petrovna, beside herself with anxiety, followed him.

"Just don't get frightened, for God's sake, Sofia Petrovna,"
he said when she'd closed the door. "Calm down, please, Sofia
Petrovna, there's really nothing to be frightened about. It's nothing terrible. The day before, the day before yesterday . . . or
when was it? well, the day before the last day off . . . Kolya was
arrested . . .''

He sat down on the sofa, and tearing his scarf off with both
hands, threw it on the floor and burst into tears.

9

S HE must rush off somewhere at once and clear up this monstrous misunderstanding. She must go immediately to Sverdlovsk and roust out lawyers, prosecutors, judges, investigators. Sofia Petrovna put on her coat, hat, and boots and got some money out of a box. She mustn't forget her passport; then to the station immediately for tickets.

But Alik, wiping his face with his scarf, said that in his opinion going to Sverdlovsk immediately made no sense at all. Kolya, as a native of Leningrad who had only recently gone to Sverdlovsk, would most probably be brought to Leningrad. Wouldn't it be better to put off her trip to Sverdlovsk for a while? What if she and Kolya should miss each other? Sofia Petrovna took off her coat and threw her passport and money on the table.

"The keys? Did you leave the keys there?" she cried suddenly, stepping towards Alik. "Did you leave the keys with someone?"

"The keys? What keys?" Alik was dumbfounded.

"Lord, how stupid you are!" said Sofia Petrovna, and suddenly burst into loud sobs. Natasha ran up to her and put her arms around her shoulders. "Yes, the keys . . . from the room . . . in your, what's-it-called . . . hostel . . ."

They didn't understand and looked at her in bewilderment. What fools! But Sofia Petrovna had a lump in her throat and couldn't speak. Natasha poured a glass of water and held it out to her.

"But he . . . but he . . ." said Sofia Petrovna, pushing away the glass, "but he's . . . they probably . . . have already released him . . . have seen he's the wrong person . . . and released him . . . he's returned home to find you gone . . . and

45

the key gone . . . Any minute there'll probably be a telegram from him.''

Sofia Petrovna lay down on her bed without taking off her boots. She wept, burying her head in her pillow, wept a long time, until both her cheeks and the pillow were wet. When she got up, her face hurt and her heart was pounding.

Natasha and Alik were whispering over by the window.

"Here's what Natalia Sergeyevna and I have decided,'' said Alik, his kind eyes looking at her pityingly from behind his glasses. ''You just go to bed now, and in the morning go quietly to the prosecutor. Natalia Sergeyevna will tell them tomorrow at the publishing house that you're ill . . . or something else . . . that you were poisoned by fumes in the night . . . I don't know what.''

Alik left. Natasha wanted to spend the night, but Sofia Petrovna said she didn't need anything, anything at all. Natasha kissed her and left. It looked as if she'd been crying, too. Sofia Petrovna washed her face with cold water, undressed and lay down. In the darkness flashes from the streetcar wires, lightning-like, lit up the room. A square white patch of light folded like a sheet of paper lay across the wall and ceiling. In the nurse's room Valya was still squealing and laughing.

Sofia Petrovna visualized Kolya being taken, under escort, to the investigator. The investigator would be a handsome military man with straps and pockets everywhere.

"You are Nikolai Fomich Lipatov?'' the military man asks Kolya.

''I am Nikolai Fyodorovich Lipatov,'' replies Kolya with dignity.

The investigator sharply reprimands the escort and presents his apologies to Kolya. "Bah!'' he says, "why didn't I recognize you at once? Why, you're that young engineer whose portrait I saw recently in *Pravda*! Please forgive me. The thing is, a person of the same last name, Nikolai Fomich Lipatov, is a Trotskyite, fascist hireling, and saboteur . . .''

All night long Sofia Petrovna lay awake waiting for a telegram. Returning home to his hostel and learning that Alik had left for Leningrad, Kolya would immediately send a telegram to reassure his mother. About six in the morning, when the streetcars had again started screeching, Sofia Petrovna fell asleep. She was awakened by a shrill ring which seemed to go straight to her heart. A telegram? But there was no second ring.

Sofia Petrovna got dressed, washed, made herself drink some tea and tidy up the room a little. Then she went out into the street, into the half-light. It was still thawing, but during the night a thin coat of ice had formed on the puddles.

After taking a few steps, Sofia Petrovna stopped. Where, actually, should she go?

Alik had said to the prosecutor's office. But Sofia Petrovna didn't know precisely what the prosecutor's office was, or where it was. She was embarrassed to ask passersby about the place. So she went not to the prosecutor's office, but to the prison, because she happened to know that the prison was on Shpalernaya Street.

Outside the iron gates stood a sentry with a rifle. The small side door near the gates was locked. Sofia Petrovna pushed the door with her hand and her knee, but to no avail. Nowhere was there any sign of a notice.

The sentry came up to her.

"At nine o'clock they'll start letting people in," he said.

It was twenty to eight. Sofia Petrovna decided not to go home. She walked back and forth outside the prison, craning her neck upwards and gazing at the iron bars.

Could it possibly be true that Kolya was here, in this building, behind those bars?

"You're not allowed to walk here, lady," said the sentry.

Sofia Petrovna crossed to the other side of the street and walked on mechanically. On her left she saw the wide, snowy expanse of the Neva.

She turned down a street to the left and came out on the embankment.

It was completely light by now. Silently, in astonishing unison, the street lights on Liteynyi bridge went out. The Neva was piled with heaps of dirty yellow snow. "They probably bring snow from all over the city here," thought Sofia Petrovna.

She noticed a large crowd of women in the middle of the street. Some were leaning against the parapet of the embankment, others walked slowly along the sidewalk or on the

47

pavement. Sofia Petrovna was surprised that they were all very warmly dressed, muffled in scarves over their coats, and almost all in felt boots and galoshes. They were stamping their feet and blowing on their hands. "They must have stood here a long time to be so cold," Sofia Petrovna reflected for lack of anything to do, "it's no longer freezing, the thaw has begun." All the women looked as though they'd been waiting for hours on end for a train at a waystation.

Sofia Petrovna took a careful look at the building across from which a crowd of women was standing—an ordinary building without any sort of sign on it. What was it they were all waiting for? In the crowd there were ladies in elegant coats and also simple women. Again for lack of anything better to do, Sofia Petrovna walked once or twice through the crowd. One woman stood there holding an infant in her arms and another child, muffled crosswise in a scarf, by the hand. Near the wall of the building there was a man standing alone. All their faces looked a little green—maybe it was the half light of the morning that made them look that way?

Suddenly a small, neatly dressed old woman with a cane walked up to Sofia Petrovna. From under her sealskin cap, pulled down low on her forehead, shone silver hair and dark, Semitic eyes.

"Do you want the list?" she said in a friendly way. "In the front hall of No. 28."

"What list?"

"For 'L' and 'M' . . . Oh, I'm sorry! You were walking here, so I thought you'd also come about someone who was arrested."

"Yes, about my son . . ." Sofia Petrovna said in bewilderment.

Turning away from the old woman, upset by her surprising perspicacity, Sofia Petrovna went to look for the main entrance of house No. 28. The thought that all these women had come here for the same reason she had filled her with vague foreboding. But why were they here, on the embankment, not outside the prison? Oh, yes, the sentry doesn't allow standing outside the prison.

House No. 28 turned out to be a rundown private mansion almost at the bridge. Sofia Petrovna went into the vestibule which was luxurious but dirty, with a fireplace, a huge broken mirror, and a marble cupid with one wing missing. On the first step of the grand staircase lay a woman curled up on a newspaper with a battered, old briefcase under her head.

"You want your name on the list?" she asked, raising her head. Then she sat up and pulled a pencil and a crumpled sheet of paper out of her briefcase.

"I . . . really don't know," said Sofia Petrovna distractedly. "I've come to speak to someone about my son, who was arrested by mistake in Sverdlovsk . . . You understand, they simply mistook him for someone else of the same name . . ."

"Lower your voice, please," the woman irritatedly interrupted her. She had an intelligent, tired face. "Lists get taken away, and anyway . . . What's the last name?"

"Lipatov," Sofia Petrovna replied timidly.

"Three forty-four," said the woman, writing it down. "Your number is three forty-four. Now, please leave."

"Three forty-four," repeated Sofia Petrovna and went out onto the embankment again.

The crowd was still growing. "What's your number?" people kept asking Sofia Petrovna.

"Then you won't get in today," said a woman muffled in a kerchief, peasant-fashion. "We all put our names on the list yesterday evening . . ."

"Where's the list?" asked others in a whisper.

It was quite light now. Day had begun.

Then suddenly the whole crowd of people began to run. Sofia Petrovna ran with them. A child bundled up in a scarf began to cry loudly. He had bandy little legs and could hardly keep up with his mother. The crowd turned down Shpalernaya Street. Sofia Petrovna saw from a distance that the small door next to the iron gates was already open. People were squeezing through it as though through a streetcar door. Sofia Petrovna squeezed through, too. And suddenly stopped: there was nowhere else to go.

The half-lit entrance hall and small wooden staircase were jammed with people. The crowd swayed back and forth. People were untying their scarves, undoing their coat collars and elbowing their way about, each trying to find the number just before and just after their own. And more and more people kept shoving in from behind. Sofia Petrovna was tossed about like a wood chip. She unbuttoned her coat and wiped her forehead with her handkerchief.

Once she had caught her breath and grown used to the semi-darkness, Sofia Petrovna also began to look for the numbers she needed: three forty-three and three forty-five. Three forty-five was a man, and three forty-three, a hunched-over, ancient woman.

"Is your husband a Latvian, too?" asked the old woman, lifting dulled eyes to Sofia Petrovna.

"No, why?" answered Sofia Petrovna. "Why Latvian specifically? My husband died a long time ago, but he was Russian."

"Excuse me, please, do you already have a travel voucher?" Sofia Petrovna was asked by the old Jewish woman with silver hair who had spoken to her on the embankment.

Sofia Petrovna didn't answer. She couldn't understand anything here. The woman lying on the staircase, and now all kinds of silly questions about Latvians and travel vouchers . . . What did travel vouchers have to do with it? She felt as if she were not in Leningrad at all, but in some unknown city. How strange to think that her job, the publishing house, Natasha tapping away at her typewriter was only half an hour's walk away . . .

Once they found the numbers next to their own, people stood quietly. Sofia Petrovna could make it out now: the staircase led up to a room which was also crowded with people, and it seemed that beyond this room was yet another. Sofia Petrovna looked around furtively. There was a woman with a briefcase, wearing woolen socks over her stockings and clumsy shoes—she was the same one who had been lying on the staircase. People kept coming up to her, but she wouldn't take their names: it was too late.

Just think of it, all these women, the mothers, wives and sisters of saboteurs, terrorists and spies! And the men, the husband or brother of one . . . They all looked perfectly ordinary, like those on a streetcar or in a store. Except they all looked tired and baggy-eyed. "I can imagine how awful it must be for a mother to learn that her son is a saboteur," thought Sofia Petrovna.

Now and then a woman would descend the narrow, creaking staircase, pushing her way with difficulty through the crowd.

"Did they accept it?" she would be asked at the bottom.

"Accepted it," and she'd show a pink slip of paper.

But one of them, looking to be a dairy woman with a large milkcan in her hand, answered, "deported!" and burst into loud sobs, setting down her milkcan and leaning her head against the doorpost. Her kerchief slipped down, revealing reddish hair and small earrings.

"Quiet!" people shushed at her from all sides. "He doesn't like noise, he'll shut the window and that will be that. Quiet!"

The dairy woman straightened her kerchief and went out with tears rolling down her cheeks.

Sofia Petrovna realized from what she heard people saying that most of these women had come to pass on money to husbands and sons who'd been arrested, and some to find out whether a husband or son was here. Sofia Petrovna's head was spinning from stuffiness and fatigue. She was very afraid that the mysterious little window which everyone was pushing toward would be closed before she got there.

"If it closes at two today, we won't make it," the man said to her.

"At two? Do we really have to stand here until two?" thought Sofia Petrovna miserably. "It can't be past ten yet."

She closed her eyes, trying to stop her dizziness. Quiet, brief conversations buzzed steadily around her.

"When did they take yours?"

"More than two months ago."

"And mine, two weeks ago."

"At the prosecutor's office. But they don't tell you anything anywhere."

"Have you been to Chaikovsky Street? What about Herzen Street?"

"Herzen Street is for the military."

"When did they take yours?"

"It was my daughter."

"They say they take clothing at Arsenalnaya Street."

"Who are you, Latvians?"

"No, we're Poles."

"When did they take yours?"

"Half a year ago already."

"What numbers have they reached?"

"Only the twenties? My God, my God, if only he won't close at two! Last time he slammed it shut at two on the dot!"

Sofia Petrovna repeated to herself what she would ask: "Had they brought Kolya to Leningrad? When could one see the judge—or what was he called, the investigator? Couldn't it be today? And couldn't she have a meeting with Kolya right away?"

After two hours Sofia Petrovna, following right after the ancient woman, reached the first step of the wooden staircase. After three, the first room. After four, the second room, and after five, following the winding line, back in the first room again. From behind she could make out a square wooden window and in the window the wide shoulders and big hands of a stout man. It was three o'clock. Sofia Petrovna counted—there were fifty-nine people ahead of her.

The women, giving the name, would timidly hand money in at the window. The bandy-legged little boy was sobbing and licking his tears away with his tongue. "Just wait till I have a talk with him," thought Sofia Petrovna impatiently. "Let him take me at once to see the investigator, to the prosecutor or whomever . . . What a lot of uncivilized things we have to put up with in our lives! It's so stuffy, yet they can't even ventilate the place. Someone ought to write a letter to *Leningrad Pravda* about it."

And then, at last, there were only three people ahead of Sofia Petrovna. She also prepared some money just in case: in the meantime, Kolya mustn't be caught short. With a trembling hand, the hunched-over old woman handed thirty rubles in at the window and received a pink slip in return. She peered at it with her weak eyes. Sofia Petrovna hurriedly took her place. She saw a stout young man with a puffy white face and small sleepy eyes.

"I want to know," began Sofia Petrovna, bending down to see the face of the man behind the window better, "whether my son is here? The thing is he was arrested by mistake . . ."

"Last name?" the man interrupted.

"Lipatov. He was arrested by mistake and I haven't heard anything in several days . . ."

"Be quiet, lady," said the man, bending over a drawer full of cards. "Lipatov or Lepatov?"

"Lipatov. I would like to see the prosecutor today or anyone you care to direct me to . . ."

"Letters?"

Sofia Petrovna did not understand.

"What's his first name?"

"Oh, his initials? N. F."

"N or M?"

"N, Nikolai."

"Lipatov, Nikolai Fyodorovich," said the man, taking a card out of the drawer. "He's here."

"I would like to know . . ."

"We don't give out information. No more conversation, lady. Next!"

Sofia Petrovna quickly reached thirty rubles through the window.

"Not allowed for him," said the man, pushing the money away.

"Next! Move on, lady, don't get in the way."

"Go away!" people whispered to Sofia Petrovna from behind. "Or he'll shut the window."

Sofia Petrovna reached home after five. In her room she found Alik and Natasha. She sank down on a chair and for several minutes didn't have the strength to take off her boots and coat. Alik and Natasha looked at her questioningly. She reported that Kolya was here, in prison, on Shpalernaya Street, but simply couldn't explain to them how it was she hadn't found out the reason for his arrest or when she'd be allowed to see him.

10

SOFIA Petrovna took two weeks' leave without pay from the publishing house. While Kolya sat in prison, she simply couldn't think about any sort of papers or about Erna Semyonovna! In any case, there wasn't time to go to the office: she had to stand in lines day and night.

She submitted her request to the lame party secretary: after the arrest of Zakharov he had been temporarily appointed acting director. He now sat in the office where Zakharov used to sit, behind the same big desk with the telephones; he no longer wore his Russian shirt, but a gray suit from the Leningrad Clothing Store, with a collar and tie—but he still looked homely.

Sofia Petrovna said that she needed the time off for personal reasons. Timofeyev spent a long time writing out a certificate in red ink without looking at her. He told Sofia Petrovna that Erna Semyonovna would take her place this time and instructed her to turn over her affairs to her.

"But why not Frolenko?" Sofia Petrovna asked in surprise. "Erna Semyonovna is not properly literate and makes mistakes in spelling . . ."

Comrade Timofeyev made no reply and stood up.

Oh well, what did it matter! Sofia Petrovna left his office. She was hurrying to get in line.

All her days and nights were now spent neither at home nor at the office, but in a kind of new world—in line. She stood on the embankment of the Neva, or on Chaikovsky Street—there were benches there, one could sit down—or in the enormous hall of the Big House,* or on the staircase in the prosecutor's office. She only went home to eat or sleep a little when Natasha or Alik took her place. (The director had given Alik permission to go to Leningrad for only one week, but he kept putting off his return to Sverdlovsk from day to day in the hope that he and Kolya would be able to return together.)

Sofia Petrovna had learned a lot of things during those two weeks: she had learned that one should go at night to get on the list, at about eleven or twelve, and appear every two hours for the roll call, though it was better not to go away at all, or else one might be stricken off the list; that it was essential to take a warm scarf and put on felt boots, because even though it was thawing, one's feet would freeze between three and six in the morning and one's whole body would shiver with cold; she learned that the lists were taken away by NKVD officials and that those who made out the lists were taken to the police station; that one must go to the prosecutor's office on the first day of the week, and there they received everyone and not in alphabetical order, whereas on Shpalernaya Street the days for her letter were the seventh and the twentieth (the first time by some miracle she had happened to hit the right day), that the families of those who had been arrested were sent out of Leningrad—the "travel vouchers" were not a pass to a sanatorium, but for deportation; that on Chaikovsky Street information was given out by a red-faced old man with a bushy moustache like a cat's, but at the prosecutor's, by a young girl with tight curls and a sharp nose; that on Chaikovsky Street you had to show your passport, but on Shpalernaya Street—not. She learned that among the unmasked enemies there were a lot of Latvians and Poles, which explained why there were so many Latvian and Polish women in the lines. She was soon able to pick out at a glance which of the people in Chaikovsky Street were not casual passersby, but were holding a place in line; even in the streetcar she could tell from their eyes which of the women were on their way to the iron gates of the prison. She became familiar with all the main and back stairs of the buildings along the embankment and could easily find the woman with the list no

---

*KGB headquarters. (Translator)

matter where she might hide. She knew now, when she left home after a short sleep, that wherever she went—on the street, on the staircase, in the corridor, in the hall, on Chaikovsky Street, on the embankment, at the prosecutor's office—there would be women, women, women, old and young, in kerchiefs and hats, alone or with small children or babies—children crying from lack of sleep and quiet, frightened, laconic women; and as in her childhood, when upon closing her eyes after an excursion to the woods she had seen nothing but berries, berries, berries, now when she closed her eyes, she saw faces, faces, faces . . .

There was only one thing she did not learn in these two weeks: Why had Kolya been arrested? Who was going to try him, and when? What was he accused of? And when would this stupid misunderstanding finally come to an end so he could return home?

At the information office on Chaikovsky Street the red-faced old man with the bushy mustache would look at her passport and ask: "What's your son's name? You're his mother? Why didn't his wife come? Not married? Lipatov, Nikolai? Being investigated," and throw her passport back through the window; and before Sofia Petrovna had time to open her mouth, the mechanical shutter on the window would drop with a bang and a bell would ring meaning: "Next!" There was no point in talking to the shutter, so after waiting a moment, Sofia Petrovna would go away.

At the prosecutor's office the young girl with the tightly curled hair and sharp nose would lean out of the window and say: "Lipatov? Nikolai Fyodorovich? The case has not yet reached the prosecutor's office. Inquire again in two weeks."

On Shpalernaya Street the stout, sleepy man invariably pushed the money aside with the words: "Not allowed for him." That was all she knew about Kolya: others were allowed money, but he for some reason was not. Why? But she already understood that questioning the person at the window was useless.

On the other hand, she would question Alik avidly about how it happened, how they took Kolya away. And Alik would obediently recount again and again how they'd already gone to sleep when suddenly there'd been a knock at the door and the dormitory manager had come in, followed by the superintendent, and

57

behind him someone in civilian clothes and another person in a military uniform.

"What time was it?" Sofia Petrovna would ask.

"Oh, about half-past one or so," Alik would reply and go on. "The superintendent turned on the light, and the civilian asked: 'Which one here is Lipatov, Nikolai?' "

"Kolya was scared?" Sofia Petrovna would interrupt with alarm.

"Not in the least," Alik would answer. "He put on his underclothes, his shirt, his suit, and asked me to tell them at the factory the next day that he'd been detained by mistake and that he might miss several days . . . Let Yasha Roitman take his place in the section . . . that's a Komsomol member who works there . . ."

"And is it true he took nothing with him, absolutely nothing?" Sofia Petrovna would anxiously clasp her hands.

Alik would explain that Kolya absolutely refused to take either a change of underwear or a towel, even though the laundress had just brought the things back. " 'What for? I'll be back tomorrow or the day after.' 'I strongly advise you to take them,' said the military man. But Kolya repeated to him, too, that there was no point, he'd be back tomorrow."

"That just shows what a clear conscience he had!" Sofia Petrovna would say with emotion. "But will they give him a towel there?"

Alik had dutifully waited for Kolya one day, two, three, and only on the fourth day had decided to go to Leningrad—to clear up the situation. He lied to the director, saying his mother was on the point of death. And the director—a good-hearted fellow—had given him permission to go.

Sofia Petrovna would question Alik closely: perhaps Kolya had quarreled with the management? been rude to someone? associated with someone who later turned out to be a saboteur? or some woman, perhaps, had entangled him in something?

"What do you mean, a woman!" Alik would answer with slight annoyance. "Nikolai entangled? Surely you know him better than that. Our director used to say quite openly of him that this is a future world-famous engineer . . ."

Yes, of course, of course, Kolya was not capable of doing anything wrong. She, Sofia Petrovna, should certainly know what a heart of gold he had, and what a brain, and how absolutely loyal he was to the Soviet regime and the party. But, at the same time, nothing happens without a reason. Kolya was still young, he'd never lived on his own. He must have put someone's back up. You have to know how to get along with people. And Sofia Petrovna would look at Alik with some hostility: he hadn't looked out for him properly. If only Kolya had stayed in Leningrad, under his mother's eye, nothing would have happened to him. She should never have let him go to Sverdlovsk.

But even so, even so, nothing terrible could happen, Sofia Petrovna went on persuading herself. Every hour, every minute, she expected Kolya to come home. On the way to get in line, she always left the key to her room on the shelf in the corridor, in the old, accustomed place. She even left hot soup ready for him in the oven. And coming back, she hurried upstairs without pausing for breath, as she used to when expecting his letters: she'd enter her room, and Kolya would be home, wondering where on earth his mother had gotten to?

The night before, in the line, one woman had said to another—Sofia Petrovna had heard her: "No point waiting for him to return! Those who wind up here never return." Sofia Petrovna had wanted to interrupt, but decided not to get involved. In our country innocent people aren't held. Particularly not Soviet patriots like Kolya. They'll clear the matter up and let him go.

One evening, having persuaded Sofia Petrovna to lie down for an hour or two, Alik put on his coat, wrapped a scarf around his neck, and said good-bye: it was the nineteenth, he was going to get in line on Shpalernaya Street.

"I'll be there no later than two," said Sofia Petrovna from her bed, in a weak voice.

"Sofia Petrovna, even at five is all right," he answered cheerfully and went out the door.

Then for some reason he came back again. He went up to Natasha who was sitting beside the window knitting. "What do you think, Natalia Sergeyevna," he asked, his bright eyes looking her straight in the face from behind his glasses, "there, in prison, are they all as guilty as Kolya? All those mothers standing in line somehow look an awful lot like Sofia Petrovna."

"I don't know," answered Natasha, in the way that was now typical of her.

Natasha had been silent before, but since Kolya had been arrested, she scarcely spoke at all. To a question she would answer "yes" or "no" or "I don't know." She spent all her time away from work with Sofia Petrovna—cooking the dinner, washing the dishes, giving her water with valerian drops— or else standing in lines. And all the time she never opened her mouth.

"But, Alik," Sofia Petrovna said quietly. "How can you compare them? After all Kolya was arrested through a misunderstanding, but the others . . . Don't you read the newspapers, or what?"

"Oh, the newspapers," replied Alik and left.

The papers had just published confessions made by the accused at their trials. In line the day before Sofia Petrovna had read a whole page over the shoulder of the man standing in front of her. Her legs were aching and her heart was heavy, but the newspaper was so interesting she craned her neck and read the whole thing. The accused told in detail about murders and poisonings and explosions and—Sofia Petrovna was as indignant as the prosecutor.

"What are such things called?" the prosecutor would ask the accused with controlled anger. "Treachery!" the accused would answer contritely.

No, Sofia Petrovna had been quite right to keep aloof from her neighbors in the lines. She was sorry for them, of course, as human beings, sorry especially for the children; but still an honest person had to remember that all these women were the wives and mothers of poisoners, spies and murderers.

60

11

Two weeks passed. Alik returned to Sverdlovsk, to his factory. Sofia Petrovna went back to the publishing house—still having found out nothing about Kolya.

The women in the line explained to her that the case would in all probability finally reach the prosecutor's office, and when a case reached the prosecutor's office then one could go to the prosecutor. He received people not through a window, but behind a desk, and one could tell him everything.

For the moment there was only one thing to do—go to the office, count the lines, smile, distribute the work, and to the clatter and ring of typewriters, think constantly of Kolya. Kolya sitting in prison, Kolya in prison. Among bandits, spies, murderers. In a cell. Locked up.

Whenever she tried to visualize the prison and Kolya in prison, she invariably thought of the picture of Princess Tarakanova: a dark wall, a girl with disheveled hair pressing up against the wall, water rising on the floor, and rats . . . but a Soviet prison, of course, was not like that at all.

Alik, when he said good-bye, advised her not to speak to anyone about Kolya's arrest.

"I've no reason to be ashamed of Kolya!" Sofia Petrovna began angrily, but then agreed with Alik: other people after all didn't know Kolya, and who knows what they might imagine. And so she said nothing to anybody either at work or in the apartment— except to Degtyarenko's wife, who found her one day weeping in the bathroom.

Degtyarenko's wife sighed sympathetically. "It's no use weeping, he may still return," she said. "Now I understand why you've been running around day and night, you don't look yourself at all.''

Five months had passed since the day of Kolya's arrest—winter had already given way to spring and spring to a fiercely hot June—and there was still no Kolya. Sofia Petrovna was worn out by the heat, the waiting, the nights in line. Five months, three weeks and four days, and five days, and six days . . .

Five months and four weeks. Kolya still had not returned, money was still "not allowed" for him, and Sofia Petrovna suddenly began to have difficulties at work. Difficulties one after another. The person responsible for these difficulties was Erna Semyonovna.

When Sofia Petrovna returned to work after her two weeks away, Erna Semyonovna remained her assistant: she had to check the typed manuscripts. Sofia Petrovna thought her no help whatsoever: since she was illiterate, how could she correct the mistakes of others? But there was no way to go against Timofeyev's decision. So Erna Semyonovna did the checking, and Sofia Petrovna said nothing.

And then one day sullen Comrade Timofeyev, rattling his keys—he now always carried with him all the keys to all the desks and all the rooms—stopped Sofia Petrovna in the corridor and asked her to send Frolenko to him after work. Sofia Petrovna sent Natasha to his office and waited for her in the cloakroom, wondering what Comrade Timofeyev could want from Natasha.

Natasha came back fairly soon. Her gray face was impassive, only her lips seemed to tremble slightly. "They've fired me," she said when they went out into the street.

Sofia Petrovna stopped short.

"Erna Semyonovna showed the party secretary the work I typed yesterday. You remember, the long article on the Red Army? In one place I had typed Ret Army, instead of Red Army."

"But wait a minute," said Sofia Petrovna, "that's a simple typing mistake. Why do you imagine you'll be fired tomorrow? Everyone knows you're the best typist in the office."

"He said they would fire me for lack of vigilance." Natasha walked on. The sun was beating right in her eyes, but she didn't lower them.

Sofia Petrovna took her home with her, and gave her tea. Kolya was not there. Before, when Kolya had been living happily in Sverdlovsk, Sofia Petrovna hadn't been miserable that he wasn't with her. She was just a bit lonely. But now everything in the room seemed to cry out at Sofia Petrovna that Kolya was gone. On the windowsill, all alone, stood his black cogwheel.

"I'll come to the publishing house tomorrow, but it'll be the last time," said Natasha as she was saying good-bye.

"Don't talk nonsense!" Sofia Petrovna called after her. "That can't happen."

But it turned out it could. The next day on the bulletin board in the corridor hung an announcement about the dismissal of N. Frolenko and E. Grigorieva, the director's former secretary. The reason given for the dismissal of Frolenko was lack of political vigilance, and for the dismissal of the secretary, association with an unmasked enemy of the people, the former director Zakharov.

Next to this announcement hung a large placard which said that today at five o'clock there would be a general meeting for all publishing house employees. The agenda: 1) Speech by Comrade Timofeyev on sabotage activities on the publishing front. 2) Other business. Attendance compulsory.

Natasha took her briefcase and left right after the bell rang, saying to everyone at once: "Good-bye." "All the best," the typists replied in chorus; only Erna Semyonovna did not answer: she was fixing her hair, looking at her reflection in the window pane. Sofia Petrovna's heart sank. She accompanied Natasha as far as the cloakroom.

"Come over this evening," she said to her in parting.

The chairman of the Mestkom was already summoning everyone to the director's office. The elevator lady Marya Ivanovna was bringing in chairs. Sofia Petrovna entered and sat down in the first row. She felt frightened and alone. The ceiling light was switched on and the heavy blinds closed. The employees were coming in and taking their places. On every face was a kind of eager, anxious curiosity.

"Do we have to send you a special invitation, comrades?" the Mestkom chairman shouted into the editorial department.

Timofeyev stood at the desk, concentrating on sorting out papers.

The Mestkom chairman declared the meeting open. She was unanimously elected, by a halfhearted show of hands, to preside over the meeting. Comrade Timofeyev cleared his throat.

"Comrades, we have met today to discuss an important matter," he began, "to cor-rob-ber-ate the existence in our publishing house of a criminal lack of vigilance and to consider together how to liquidate its consequences." He spoke confidently and smoothly this time, almost without stammering. "For five whole years right here, under our very noses, if one may use such an expression, there operated in our collective an individual now exposed as an enemy of the people, an evil bandit, terrorist, and saboteur, the former director Zakharov. Zakharov has now been deprived of the opportunity to do sabotage. But in his time he brought along with him a whole train of puppets, his retinue, if I may put it like that, who with him built a solid nest in our midst and in all manner of ways helped him in his filthy Trotskyite machinations. To the shame of our collective. Zakharov's retinue has still not been liquidated. I have here in front of me"—he spread out the papers—"I have here in front of me documentary data, which will give you documentary proof of their filthy counterrevolutionary activities.

Timofeyev paused and poured himself some water.

"What do these documents show?" he began again, wiping his mouth with the palm of his hand. "This document here shows irrefutably that in 1932 on the personal order of the director, without consultation with the Mestkom and the personnel department, on the, I repeat, personal order of the director, a certain Frolenko was hired."

Sofia Petrovna shrank back in her chair, as if he'd begun to speak of her.

"And who is this Frolenko? She's the daughter of a colonel who under the old regime was the owner of a so-called estate. What, it is asked, was citizeness Frolenko doing in our publishing house, the daughter of an alien element, appointed to her job by the bandit Zakharov? Another document will tell us about that. Under the wing of Zakharov, citizeness Frolenko learned to blacken our beloved Red Army of workers and peasants, to strike counterrevolutionary blows: she calls the Red Army, the *Rat* Army . . ."

Sofia Petrovna felt her mouth go dry.

"And the former secretary Grigorieva? She was the director's loyal accomplice, on whom he could rely in all his, if I may say so, activity.

"How did it happen that this saboteur and his hangers-on for five whole years insolently bamboozled Soviet society? This, comrades, can be explained by one thing only: the criminal relaxation of political vigilance."

Comrade Timofeyev sat down and began to drink some water. Sofia Petrovna looked longingly at the water: how dry her mouth and throat were. The Mestkom chairman rang the bell sharply, although everyone was silent and no one stirred.

"Who wishes to speak?" she asked.

Silence.

"Comrades, who wishes the floor?" the Mestkom chairman asked again.

Silence.

"Can it possibly be that no one wants to say a few words on such a burning issue?"

Silence. Then suddenly a loud voice from the door, at which everyone turned around. It was the elevator lady, Marya Ivanovna. Up till now she hadn't spoken at a single meeting. Indeed, few people at the publishing house had ever heard her voice.

"Please, please, this way, Comrade Ivanovna!"

The elevator woman walked heavily up to the desk.

"Well, I want to have my proletarian say in this, too. About the secretary, that's right citizens. Like, it used to be, she'd get in the elevator in galoshes—dirt, dirt everywhere—and you've got to wipe up after her. She tracks it in, and you wipe it up. You take her up, and she wants to be taken down, too. A hundret times she goes up, and then take her down, too. And you can't not take her down, when she always gets herself next to the director. Wherever he goes, she goes, too. He's in the clevator, and she's behind him, he's in the car, and she's right next to him. It's true they worked hand in hand . . . Only I want to say to Comrade Timofeyev—in our own way, in simple proletarian words—no matter how often you try to tell him: stop that fine lady! he don't pay no attention—just waves his hand and walks away. You think the elevator woman's just a little person, Comrade Timofeyev, that she don't understand? Well, you're wrong! It's not the old days now! Under Soviet rule there aren't no little people, everyone's big."

"You're right, Comrade Ivanovna, you're right," said Anna Grigorievna. "Who else would like to speak?"

Silence.

"May I," asked Sofia Petrovna quietly. She stood up, then sat down again. "I would like to say just a few words, about Frolenko . . . Certainly, it was dreadful, dreadful, what she wrote. But everyone can make mistakes in his work, isn't that true? She wrote not *Red* but *Ret* simply because on the typewriter—as every typist knows—the letter 't' is not far from the letter 'd.' Comrade Timofeyev said she wrote *Rat*, but she didn't, she wrote *Ret*, which is not quite the same thing . . . Frolenko is a highly qualified typist and very conscientious. This was simply an accident."

Sofia Petrovna fell silent.

"Are you going to reply?" The Mestkom chairman asked Timofeyev.

"Documents," answered Timofeyev from behind the table, rapping the papers with his knuckles. "You can't go against documents, Comrade Lipatova. Rat or Ret—it's all the same. An obvious act of class hostility on the part of citizeness Frolenko."

"Does anyone else wish to speak? . . . I declare the meeting closed."

People dispersed quickly, hurrying home. From near the coatrack in the cloakroom already came the buzz of conversation: about how rarely the No. 5 streetcar ran, about the excellent wool leggings which had appeared in the children's department of the Arcade Store. The accountant was inviting Erna Semyonovna to go boating with him.

"You and your boating!" she said, pursing her lips at the mirror as if for a kiss. "Now, going to the movies would be all right."

About the meeting, about sabotage activities—not a single word.

66

Sofia Petrovna walked home quickly, without even noticing the way. She had an idea that when she got back to her room and closed the door, her head would stop aching, all this would come to an end, and she would feel all right. Her temples were throbbing. Why was her head aching so?—after all no one at the meeting, it seemed, had been smoking. Poor Natasha! She had such an unlucky life! A first-class typist and suddenly . . .

In her room, on Kolya's little table, lay a note:

Dear Sofia Petrovna,

I've come back again. Yasha Roitman reported me to the Komsomol for being associated with Nikolai. I've been expelled from the Komsomol because I wouldn't dissociate myself from Nikolai and was dismissed from my job. It's very hard to be expelled from the ranks. I'll drop in tomorrow.

Yours,
Aleksandr Finkelstein

Sofia Petrovna turned the note over in her hands. My God! so many unpleasant things all at once! First Kolya, then Natasha, and now Alik. But Alik was probably himself to blame: said something foolish there at some meeting. He'd become so short-tempered. The day he left, when she again asked him, tactfully, whether Kolya might not have got into bad company, he had flushed scarlet and jamming himself up against the wall shouted at her: "Do you realize what you're asking, or don't you? Kolya's not guilty of anything, what's the matter with you—do you doubt that, or something?"

Of course, she had absolutely no doubts at all, it was silly even to say such a thing, but hadn't Kolya given some cause for offense? . . . And now, probably, Alik had said something insolent to his superiors at a meeting. Certainly, he must stick up for Kolya, but somehow carefully, tactfully, with restraint.

Sofia Petrovna's head ached. She felt as if the meeting were still going on. Timofeyev's voice rang in her ears. She felt she couldn't breathe—as though Timofeyev's voice were constricting her chest. Should she lie down? No, that wouldn't do any good. She decided to take a bath.

There had been something in Timofeyev's words that made her feel frozen, rigid. She went to get wood from the storeroom herself and heated the water tank. Before Kolya always used to bring her the wood, then Alik began getting it, and after Alik had gone back to Sverdlovsk for the second time—Natasha.

Oh, that Alik! Of course he was a good boy and devoted to Kolya, but so awfully abrupt! One mustn't shoot from the shoulder like that. Couldn't it be because of his impetuosity that Kolya was now in jail? In the line once, on Shpalernaya Street, when she had told Alik that they had again refused to take money for Kolya, he had burst out loudly: "damned bureaucrats." He could have done something like that in Sverdlovsk, at the factory.

Sofia Petrovna turned on the water, undressed and got into the tub, the one Fyodor Ivanovich had bought. She didn't feel like washing. She lay there, unmoving, with her eyes closed. What would it be like for her now at the office without Natasha? And that Erna Semyonovna! To think there should be such envious, malicious people in the world! Well, never mind, Natasha would find herself another job, somewhere not far away, and they would see each other often. If only Kolya would return soon.

She lay there looking at her hands blurred by the water. Could it really be that the secretary of the director was a saboteur? Better not to think about it. What a difficult day it had been. As before the thought of the meeting constricted her chest. She lay there with her eyes closed, in the warmth and the peace.

In the kitchen someone put out the primus stove, and the sound of voices and the clatter of dishes became immediately audible. The nurse, as usual, was saying something spiteful.

"So far I'm neither crazy nor blind," she was saying slowly. "I personally bought three liters of kerosene two days ago. And now there's just a drop left on the bottom, not enough to stick up a dog's ass. You just can't leave anything in the kitchen anymore."

"Who's going to take your kerosene?" answered Degtyarenko's wife in a low voice. One could hear by her voice that she was bending down—washing the floor or stoking the stove. "We've all got enough kerosene of our own. Me, do you think?"

"It's not you I'm talking about. There are other people besides you living in this apartment. If one member of a family's in jail—then you can expect just about anything from the others. You don't get put in prison for doing good."

Sofia Petrovna's heart stopped beating.

"So what if the son's in prison?" said Degtyarenko's wife. "He'll sit for a while, and then they'll let him out. He's not a pickpocket of some kind, not a thief. A well-educated young man. All sorts of people get put in prison these days. My husband says lots of decent people are being taken now. But they even wrote in the paper about this one. He was a famous shockworker*."

"Some shockworker! Masquerading, that's all," came Valya's voice.

"So she thinks he's some kind of innocent lamb," the nurse began again. "Excuse me, please, but people don't get locked up for nothing in our country. Enough of this. They haven't locked me up, have they? And why not? Because I'm an honest woman, a real Soviet citizen."

Sofia Petrovna went completely cold in the bath. Shivering all over, she dried herself off, threw on her bathrobe and tiptoed to her room. She lay down under her quilt and put a pillow on top, on her feet. But the shivering didn't stop. She lay there, trembling and staring straight ahead into the darkness.

About two o'clock at night, when everyone else was asleep, she got up, threw on her nightgown and coat, and made her way to the kitchen. She collected her kerosene can, her primus stove, her pots and brought them all back with her to her room.

It was nearly morning before she at last fell asleep.

---

*An exceptionally good worker. (Translator)

12

THE next day Alik was waiting for her near the entrance to the publishing house. It turned out that he and Natasha, without saying anything to her lest she worry unnecessarily, had stood in line outside the prosecutor's office since early morning. Taking turns, they had stood in line for six hours, and a half hour ago the young lady at the window had told them that the case of Nikolai Lipatov was in the hands of Prosecutor Tsvetkov. They had then taken a place for Sofia Petrovna in the line for Prosecutor Tsvetkov. Room No. 7.

Alik tried to persuade Sofia Petrovna to go home and have something to eat, but she was afraid to lose her place in the line and walked quickly, as fast as she could. She was on her way to save Kolya. His fate depended on what she was now about to say to the prosecutor. She hurried on, gasping for breath, thinking over her speech as she went. She would tell the prosecutor how Kolya had joined the Komsomol as a young boy, almost against his mother's wishes; how hard he had studied in school and at the institute, how highly they had regarded him at the factory, how he had been praised in *Pravda*, the central organ of the party. He was a fine engineer, a loyal Komsomol member, a devoted son. How could such a person possibly be suspected of sabotage or counterrevolution? What nonsense, what a wild idea! She, his old mother, had come to testify before the judge that it was not true.

Alik opened the heavy door and she went in.

In the past few months Sofia Petrovna had seen many lines, but never one like this. People were standing, sitting and lying on every step, every landing, and every ledge of the enormous, five-story staircase. It was not possible to climb this staircase without stepping on someone's hand or someone's stomach. In the corridor, near the little window and the door to Room No. 7, people were standing as crowded together as on a streetcar. These were the lucky ones who had already finished standing on the staircase. Natasha was standing hunched over against the wall beneath a large placard which read: "Up with the banner of revolutionary legality." Having made their way to her, Sofia Petrovna and Alik stopped and both took a deep breath. Alik took off his steam-clouded glasses and began to wipe them with his fingers.

"Well, I'll go now," Natasha said right away. "You're behind this lady."

Sofia Petrovna wanted to tell Natasha about yesterday's meeting, and about the way she had spoken in her defense, but Natasha's back was already disappearing in the distance, near the stairs.

"Things are bad for Natalia Sergeyevna," said Alik, motioning after Natasha with his chin. "They won't hire her anywhere. Like me."

It seemed Natasha had already managed to apply to several establishments which needed typists, but none of them had accepted her after making inquiries at her previous place of employment. Alik had also dropped by an engineering office, right on his way from the station, but when they found out he'd been expelled from the Komsomol, they wouldn't even talk to him.

"We've been put on the blacklist, as I understand it. Scoundrels! Where the hell did so many swine come from all of a sudden?" said Alik.

"Alik!" exclaimed Sofia Petrovna reprovingly. "How can you talk like that? It's that kind of language that got you expelled from the Komsomol."

"It wasn't for sharp words, Sofia Petrovna," answered Alik, and his lips trembled. "It was because I wouldn't renounce Nikolai."

"No, no, Alik," said Sofia Petrovna softly, touching him on the sleeve. "You're still very young, I assure you, you're mistaken. It's all a question of tact. For instance, yesterday I defended Natalia Sergeyevna at the meeting. And the result? Nothing's happened to me because of it. Believe me, this business with Kolya is a nightmare to me. I'm his mother. But I understand it's a temporary misunderstanding, exaggerations, disagreement . . . One has to be patient. But you start right away: scoundrels! swine! Remember what Kolya always said— we've still a lot that's not worked out yet, a lot of red tape.''

Alik said nothing. His face had frozen in a stubborn obstinate expression. He was unshaven, his face was pinched and there were dark circles under his eyes. His eyes looked out in a new way from behind his glasses: fixed and gloomy.

''I've already sent a petition to the district committee. And if they don't reinstate me there, I'm going to Moscow. Straight to the Central Committee of the Komsomol,'' he said.

''Poor boy!'' thought Sofia Petrovna. ''It will be difficult for him while he's out of work. His aunt is probably already reproaching him.'' And Sofia Petrovna, bending toward Alik, whispered: ''Watch, when they release Kolya, you'll be reinstated right away.'' And she smiled at him. But Alik did not smile back.

It was still a long way to the prosecutor's door. Sofia Petrovna counted about forty people. They went in two at a time—in Room No. 7 there were two prosecutors who received people, not just one—but all the same the line moved slowly. Sofia Petrovna examined the faces around her: it seemed to her she'd seen most of these women before—on Shpalernaya Street or Chaikovskaya Street or here at the prosecutor's office near the window. Maybe these were the same ones, or maybe they were different. There was something similar in the faces of all the women who stood in the lines outside the prisons: exhaustion, resignation, and perhaps, a certain secretiveness. Many of them were holding white slips of paper—Sofia Petrovna knew that these were deportation ''vouchers.'' In this line three questions were heard all the time: ''Where are you going?'' or ''When are you going?'' or ''Have you had a confiscation?''

Sofia Petrovna leaned against the wall and closed her eyes for a moment. What a heartless, malicious, stupid woman the wife of the accountant was. To imagine that Kolya was a saboteur! Why, she'd known him since childhood. Sofia Petrovna would never, never set foot in the kitchen again. Not until that nurse begged her forgiveness. Imagine how ashamed she'd be when

Kolya returned! Sofia Petrovna would tell Kolya everything—about his wonderful friends Natasha and Alik (without them she simply couldn't have coped with the lines) and about that snake, the wife of the accountant. Let him learn what harpies there are in this world.

When she opened her eyes, Sofia Petrovna noticed a little girl crouching down against the wall. The little girl was wearing a coat, buttoned all the way up. "How we do bundle up our children," Sofia Petrovna thought to herself, "even in summer." Then suddenly, looking more closely, she recognized the girl: it was the little daughter of the director, Zakharov. The little girl was fidgeting with her back against the wall and whimpering, bothered by the heat. And the tall, slender woman in the light-colored suit behind whom Sofia Petrovna and Alik had been standing for over an hour—she must be the wife of the director. Yes, it was she.

"How's your trumpet, not broken yet?" Sofia Petrovna asked gently, leaning down toward the child. "Or have you torn the tassel off already? Do you remember me? At the New Year's party? Let me unbutton your collar for you."

The little girl was silent, looking at Sofia Petrovna with round eyes and tugging her mother's hand.

"What's the matter? Answer the lady!" said the wife of the director.

"I knew your husband," Sofia Petrovna turned to her. "I work at the publishing house."

"Ah!" said the wife of the director, painfully twisting her lips. She wore lipstick, but it was applied beyond the outline of the lips themselves. A beautiful woman, no doubt about that—but Sofia Petrovna no longer found her as young and elegant as she had been six months before, when she used to stop in at the office to see her husband and in the corridor would graciously return the bows of the staff.

"What's happened to your husband?" inquired Sofia Petrovna.

"Ten years at remote camps."

"Then he was guilty after all. I never would have believed it. Such a nice person," thought Sofia Petrovna.

"And they're sending her and me to Kazakhstan—to some village or mountain hamlet, or something. We leave tomorrow. I'll starve to death there without work."

She spoke loudly, in a sharp voice, and everyone turned to look at her.

"And where did they send your husband?" asked Sofia Petrovna to change the subject.

"How should I know? Do you think they tell you where?"

"But then how will you . . . in ten years . . . when he's released . . . how will you find each other? You won't know his address, nor he, yours."

"And do you think," said the wife of the director, "that any one of them"—she gestured at the crowd of women with the "travel vouchers"—"knows where her husband is? The husbands have already been taken away, or will be taken tomorrow or are being taken today, the wives, too, will go off to some hellhole and haven't the foggiest idea how they're going to find their husbands later. How should I know? No one knows and neither do I."

"You have to be persistent," said Sofia Petrovna quietly. "If they won't tell you here, you must write to Moscow. Or else, what's going to happen? You'll lose track of each other completely."

The director's wife looked her up and down.

"Who is it? Your husband? Your son?" she asked with such intense fury that Sofia Petrovna involuntarily drew back closer to Alik. "All right then, when they send your son away—you just be persistent, you go find out his address."

"They won't send my son away," said Sofia Petrovna apologetically. "You see, he's not guilty. He was arrested by mistake."

"Ha-ha-ha!" laughed the director's wife, carefully enunciating each syllable. "Ha-ha-ha! By mistake!" and suddenly tears poured from her eyes. "Here, you know, everything's by mistake. . . . Oh, stand still, won't you!" she shouted at the child and bent over her to hide her tears.

There were now five people between Sofia Petrovna and the door. Sofia Petrovna repeated to herself the words she would say to the prosecutor. She thought with condescending pity about the director's wife. That's husbands for you! They make trouble, and their wives suffer for it. She's going to Kazakhstan now, with the child, and all these lines—it's enough to make anyone a nervous wreck.

"Listen, I'll go with you," said Alik suddenly. "As a colleague and friend. I'll tell the comrade prosecutor that in Nikolai we had an absolutely pure and honest person, an indomitable Bolshevik. I'll tell him about how our factory adopted the use of the Fellows' cogwheel cutter, which we owe exclusively to the inventiveness of Nikolai."

But Sofia Petrovna didn't want Alik to go to the prosecutor. She was afraid of his impetuosity: he'd say something insolent and ruin everything. No, better that she go herself. She persuaded Alik that the prosecutor would receive relatives only.

At last her turn came. The director's wife opened the door and entered. Sofia Petrovna, her heart sinking, followed her in.

Against opposite walls of a large, dark, empty room stood two desks and in front of each, a tattered armchair. Behind the desk on the right sat a portly, fair-skinned man with blue eyes. Behind the desk on the left, a hunchback. The director's wife and little girl went up to the fair-skinned man, Sofia Petrovna to the hunchback. She had long ago heard in the lines that Prosecutor Tsvetkov was a hunchback.

Tsvetkov was talking on the telephone. Sofia Petrovna sank down in the chair.

Tsvetkov was short and thin, and dressed in a greasy navy-blue suit. His head was narrow and pointed, his hump, large and round. His long wrists and fingers were covered with black hair. The way he held the telephone receiver was somehow more ape-like than human. Altogether, he looked so much like an ape to Sofia Petrovna that she found herself thinking: if he wanted to scratch behind his ear, he'd no doubt use his foot.

"Fedorov?" shouted Tsvetkov hoarsely into the receiver. "Tsvetkov here, hello. Tell Panteleev there I've got it all wrapped up. Let him send it. What? I said—let him send it."

At the other table the portly, fair-skinned man with bright blue china doll-like eyes and small, plump feminine hands was conversing politely with the director's wife.

"I'm asking you to change me from a village to some sort of city," she was saying in a jerky voice, standing in front of the desk and holding the little girl by the hand. "In a village I'll be without work. I'll have no way to feed my child and my mother. I'm a stenographer. In a village there's no stenographic work to be done. I ask you to send me not to a village, but to a city, even if it's one in that same—what do you call it?—Kazakhstan."

"Take a seat, citizeness," said the fair-skinned man gently.

"What do you want?" Tsvetkov asked Sofia Petrovna, putting down the receiver and glancing at her with his little black eyes.

"I'm here about my son. His name is Lipatov. He was arrested through a misunderstanding, by mistake. I was told you were handling his case."

"Lipatov?" repeated Tsvetkov, pausing to recollect. "Ten years at remote camps." And he picked up the telephone receiver again. "Section A? 244-16."

"What? He's already been tried?" exclaimed Sofia Petrovna. "244-16? Call Morozova."

Sofia Petrovna fell silent, her hand on her heart. Her heart beat slowly, infrequently, and loudly. The pounding resounded in her ears and in her temples. Sofia Petrovna decided to wait until Tsvetkov at last finished talking on the telephone. She looked in terror at his long, hairy wrists, his hump covered with dandruff, his yellow, unshaven face. Patience, patience. And she listened to the pounding of her heart: in her temples and in her ears.

And at the desk opposite the fair-skinned prosecutor was saying softly to the director's wife: "There's no need for you to get upset, citizeness. Take a seat, please. As a representative of legality, it is my duty to remind you that the great Stalin constitution guarantees everyone, without exception, the right to work. Since no one is depriving you of any civil rights, you are guaranteed the right to work no matter where you may be living."

The director's wife stood up quickly and went to the door. With small, unsteady steps, the little girl ran after her.

"You're still here? What do you want?" Tsvetkov asked crudely, putting down the receiver at last.

"I would like to know what my son could have been guilty of," asked Sofia Petrovna, making a supreme effort to keep her voice from trembling. "He has always been an irreproachable Komsomol member, a loyal citizen . . ."

"Your son has confessed to his crimes. The investigation is in possession of his signature. He is a terrorist and took part in terrorist activity. Do you understand?"

Tsvetkov began opening and closing the drawers of his desk. Pulling them out and slamming them shut. The drawers were empty.

Sofia Petrovna tried desperately to remember what else it was she wanted to ask. But she'd forgotten everything. And anyway in this room, in front of this person, all words were to no avail. She stood up and made her way to the door.

"How can I find out where he is now?" she asked from the door.

"That doesn't concern me."

Loyal Alik was waiting for her in the corridor. Silently they squeezed their way through the crowd in the corridor, and then down the stairs. Silently they went out into the street. In the street the streetcar bells clanged, the sun shone brightly, passersby pushed each other. The hot, stuffy summer day was still far from over.

"Well, what, Sofia Petrovna, what?" Alik asked anxiously.

"Sentenced. To remote camps. For ten years."

"You're joking!" shouted Alik. "Whatever for?"

"Taking part in terrorist activity."

"Kolya—terrorist activity! Raving nonsense!"

"The prosecutor says he himself confessed. The investigation is in possession of his signature." ·

Tears streamed down Sofia Petrovna's cheeks. She stopped near a wall, clutching a drainpipe.

"Kolya Lipatov—a terrorist!" said Alik, choking on the words. "They're swine, utter swine! It's fantastic nonsense! You know, Sofia Petrovna, I'm beginning to think that this is all some kind of colossal plot. Saboteurs have gotten themselves into the NKVD, and they're running the show. They themselves are the enemies of the people."

"But Kolya confessed, Alik, he confessed, understand, Alik, understand . . ." sobbed Sofia Petrovna.

Alik took Sofia Petrovna firmly by the arm and led her home. Outside the door of the apartment, while she was searching in her bag for the key, he began again:

"Kolya had nothing to confess to, surely you can't doubt that, can you? I don't understand anything any more, nothing at all. There's only one thing I'd like to do now: talk to Comrade Stalin face to face. Let him explain to me what he makes of all this . . ."

13

S OFIA Petrovna lay awake the whole night, her eyes open. How
many nights had it been now since Kolya's arrest—endless,
interminable? She already knew it all by heart: the summertime
shuffling of feet under the window, the shouts from the beer hall
next door, the rumble of the streetcar, dying out—then a short
silence, a short period of darkness—and again a pale dawn
filtering in the window, another new day beginning, another day
without Kolya.

Where was Kolya now, what was he sleeping on, how was he,
who was he with? Not for a moment did Sofia Petrovna doubt his
innocence: terrorist activity? Raving nonsense!—as Alik said.
He must have come up against an overzealous investigator who
confused him and made him lose his head. And Kolya wasn't
able to clear himself, he was still very young, after all.

Toward morning when it was beginning to get light again,
Sofia Petrovna finally remembered the word she'd been trying to
think of all night: "alibi." She'd read about it somewhere. He'd
simply been unable to produce his alibi.

During the first hours at the office she seemed to feel a little
better somehow. The sun was shining brightly, dust danced in
the sunbeams, and the typewriters clattered so busily—and the
typists during the lunch break ran downstairs, into the street,
then endlessly sucked ice cream on sticks—everything was so
ordinary. . . . For ten years! Now in the light of day, it became
clear what rubbish this all was. She would not see Kolya for ten
years! Why on earth? What hideous nonsense! It couldn't be.
One fine day—very soon—everything would return to normal:
Kolya would be at home, he'd argue as before with Alik about

cars and locomotives, drawing plans again—only this time she wouldn't let him go to Sverdlovsk no matter what. There were jobs available in Leningrad, too.

During the lunch break she went out into the corridor to stretch her legs; she was afraid she'd fall asleep if she stayed at her desk. A new wall newspaper hung in the corridor. A crowd of employees had gathered around it. Sofia Petrovna went up to read it also. It was a large, special issue, with red letters at the beginning of each paragraph and portraits of Lenin and Stalin on both sides of the bright red title, "Our Way." Sofia Petrovna came up to the newspaper.

"How was it possible that saboteurs for five whole years were able to engage in their filthy activities with impunity under the very nose of Soviet society?" Sofia Petrovna read. It was the editorial by Timofeyev.

In the next column was the beginning of an article by the Mestkom chairman. Anna Grigorievna made a caustic attack on Timofeyev on the grounds that his speech at the meeting had not been sufficiently self-critical. If the collective had allowed sabotage activities to pass unnoticed, then the one responsible for it must be Comrade Timofeyev, the former party secretary. Especially since, as it now became clear, the party secretary had received timely warnings from below: warning had been given by Comrade Ivanovna, who had long ago smelled out the director's secretary with her proletarian sense.

Sofia Petrovna cast her eyes over the next column. And before she grasped the meaning of what she was reading, she suddenly flushed hot inside. The article was about her, about Sofia Petrovna, about how she had spoken in defense of Natasha. The author, whose identity was concealed by the pseudonym "X," wrote:

> A scandalous occurrence took place at the meeting, for which, in our opinion, insufficient raps over the knuckles have been administered. Comrade Lipatova came out with a real speech of defense—and whom did she deem it necessary to defend? Frolenko, a colonel's daughter, who had permitted herself a gross anti-Soviet jibe at our beloved Red Army of workers and peasants. It is known that Comrade Lipatova

constantly favored Frolenko, gave her overtime work, went to the movies with her, and so on, etc. At present when the publishing house is about to enlist all the efforts of honest workers and of party and non-party Bolsheviks in order to liquidate with all possible speed the consequences of the "management" of Gerasimov-Zakharov & Co.—is it permissible, at this crucial moment, that such persons should remain on the staff of our publishing house? Up with the banner of Bolshevik vigilance, as we are taught by the genius of the leader of the peoples, Comrade Stalin! Let us root out all saboteurs, secret and open, and all those in sympathy with them!

The bell rang, signifying the end of the lunch break. Sofia Petrovna went back to her office. How was it that she hadn't noticed before that everyone was looking at her in a peculiar way today?

Back at home, she buried her head in her pillow—her last refuge. And sleep immediately closed her eyes for her. She slept a long time and dreamed about Kolya. He was wearing a fluffy gray sweater. He had attached skate blades to his boots. And then, bending low, he began skating along the corridor of the publishing house. When she awoke, the blue of dusk was already falling outside, but the light was on in her room. Natasha was sitting at the table sewing. It was obvious that she had been sewing there a long time.

"Come and sit here, nearer to me," said Sofia Petrovna in a faint voice, licking the taste of daytime sleep from her lips.

Natasha obediently brought her chair over to the head of the bed and sat down.

"You know, Kolya's been sentenced to ten years. Alik has no doubt already told you?"

Natasha nodded.

"Oh, yes, something else," Sofia Petrovna remembered. "They wrote about me in the wall newspaper, claiming I defend saboteurs and that there was no place for me in the publishing house . . ."

"Alik has been arrested. Last night," answered Natasha.

14

I F Sofia Petrovna didn't sleep at night, every hour and minute
was exactly the same to her. The light hurt her eyes, her legs
ached, and there was a gnawing feeling in her heart. But if she
did manage to sleep at night, the worst moment, without a doubt,
was the moment just after she woke up. When she opened her
eyes and caught sight of the window, the bottom of the bed,
her dress hanging over the chair—for a second she thought of
nothing but these objects. She recognized them: window, chair,
dress. But in the next second somewhere in the neighborhood of
her heart arose a feeling of dread, like a pain, and through the
haze of that pain she would suddenly remember everything:
Kolya had been sentenced to ten years, Natasha had been fired,
Alik had been arrested, and she'd been written up as being hand
in glove with saboteurs. Yes, also—the kerosene.

At the office she no longer talked with anyone. She didn't even
say a word when she set down before the typists papers brought
to her for typing. And no one talked with her. From behind her
desk in the office, she scrutinized the faces of the typists, trying
to guess who had written about her in the newspaper. Most likely
of all was Erna Semyonovna. But could she really write so
smoothly? And when was it she'd seen her and Natasha at the
movies? They hadn't seen her once.

One day, when she was loitering in a melancholy way in the
corridor, she almost bumped into Natasha. Natasha looked like a
sleepwalker, picking her way carefully as though in darkness.

"Natasha, what are you doing here?" asked Sofia Petrovna,
startled.

"I've read the newspaper. Don't speak to me. They'll see," Natasha answered her.

That evening she came to see Sofia Petrovna. Now she seemed excited and talked incessantly, jumping from one subject to another. Sofia Petrovna had never before heard Natasha talk so much. And this time she did not embroider or sew.

"What do you think, is Kolya still here in the city or far away already?" she asked suddenly.

"I don't know, Natasha," answered Sofia Petrovna with a sigh. "On Shpalernaya Street the day for his letter is the twentieth, and today is only the tenth."

"No, I don't mean that. What do you feel about it?" Natasha made a gesture in the air. "Is he still here, close to us, or is he already far away? I think he's far away. Yesterday I suddenly had the feeling that he was already far away. He's no longer here . . . And you know, Sofia Petrovna, the elevator woman refused to take me up in the elevator. 'I don't have to take just anybody up . . .' Yes, Sofia Petrovna, you must leave the publishing house right now, tomorrow. Promise me you'll leave. My dear, please promise! Tomorrow, all right?"

Natasha knelt on the couch where Sofia Petrovna was sitting and clasped her hands entreatingly before her. Then she sat down at the table, took a pen and herself wrote a letter of resignation in Sofia Petrovna's name. She assured Sofia Petrovna that it was essential that she leave of her own free will, otherwise they would surely dismiss her for associating with saboteurs—"that's with me," said Natasha, her pale lips smiling—and then she wouldn't be able to find work anywhere.

Sofia Petrovna signed the letter of resignation. She had already been thinking about leaving. Things had somehow become terrifying at the publishing house. The very sight of Timofeyev limping along with the bunch of keys in his hand sent cold shivers down her back.

"I won't be able to work in Leningrad anyway," she said sadly. "I'll be deported anyway. All wives and mothers get sent away."

"What do you think?" asked Natasha, taking a book off the shelf and replacing it immediately. "How do you explain the fact Kolya confessed? You can trip a person up, confuse him, I understand that, but only in small things. How could Kolya have been brought to the point of confessing to a crime he never committed? No matter what you say, I simply can't understand that. And why do they all confess? All the wives are told their husbands confessed. . . . Were they all tripped up?"

"He simply wasn't able to establish his alibi," said Sofia Petrovna. "Don't forget, Natasha, he's still very young."

"And why was Alik arrested?"

"Oh, Natasha, if you only knew the kind of crude language he used in front of everyone in line. I'm sure now that his tongue was the undoing of Kolya, too."

Natasha got ready to leave. As she said good-bye, she suddenly embraced Sofia Petrovna.

"What's the matter with you today?" asked Sofia Petrovna.

"With me, nothing. . . . Sit still, don't get up, it's not necessary! How much you look like Kolya, I mean, Kolya looks like you. . . . You'll submit that letter of resignation tomorrow, won't you? You won't change your mind?" she asked, looking Sofia Petrovna right in the eye. "And then—don't forget the thirtieth is the letter 'F,' you've absolutely got to transmit some money for Alik, he hasn't a cent, and his aunt will be too scared to take it. . . . And another thing, my dear, I beseech you—go to the doctor! I beg you! You don't look like yourself at all!"

"What's the use of a doctor. . . . It's Kolya," said Sofia Petrovna and dropped her eyes, which were filling with tears.

The next morning she went straight to the director's office and laid her resignation wordlessly on the glass-topped desk. Timofeyev read it through and nodded, also without a word. All the formalities were completed with amazing speed. Within two hours the announcement was posted on the wall. Within three, the polite accountant had paid her her final wages.

"You're leaving us? Ay-ay-ay, that's no good! Mind you come see us, don't forget your old friends."

For the last time she walked along the corridor. "Good-bye," she said to the typists after the bell, when they were all banging down the lids of their Underwoods.

"All the best!" they answered her in chorus as they had Natasha not long before, and one even came up to Sofia Petrovna and shook her hand warmly. Sofia Petrovna was very touched: what a courageous, noble girl that was!

"Good luck!" cried Erna Semyonovna gaily, and Sofia Petrovna no longer had the least doubt that Erna Semyonovna and no one else had written the article.

She went out into the street, into the din and clamor of the summer day. The sun was scorching down. No more going to the office—that was finished forever. She started for home, but soon turned around and headed for Natasha's instead. On every street corner small boys held out bouquets of bluebells and daisies in sweaty fingers. But because Kolya was in prison or traveling somewhere to the rumbling of wheels—the whole world had become meaningless and incomprehensible.

Climbing the stairs—Lord, it was more difficult every day to climb stairs!—reaching the fifth floor, she rang the bell. The door was opened by Natasha's neighbor, who was wiping her wet hands on her apron.

"Natalia Sergeyevna was taken to the hospital this morning," said the woman in a loud whisper. "Poisoned herself. With veronal. Mechnikov Hospital."

Sofia Petrovna backed away. The woman slammed the door.

Streetcar 17 was a long time coming. Two 9's passed and two 22's, but still no 17. Then a 17 came crawling along, barely moving, stopping at every red light. Sofia Petrovna had to stand. All the seats were taken, even the ones reserved for mothers with children, and when the ninth mother with a baby got on, no one would give her a seat.

"Soon they'll take over the whole car!" cried an old woman with a walking-stick. "They get to ride to and fro! In our day, we had to lug our children around in our arms. Carry it a while, won't kill you!"

Sofia Petrovna's knees were shaking—from fright, from the heat, from the old woman's nasty shouting. Finally she got off the bus. For some reason, she was sure Natasha was already dead.

The hospital glittered at her with all its clean-washed windows. She entered the cool white vestibule. Near the information window was a line—three people. Sofia Petrovna didn't feel she could go to the head of the line. A pretty nurse in a starched white uniform was giving out information. Near her, in front of the telephone, was a bunch of bluebells in a glass.

"Hello, hello!" she shouted into the telephone upon hearing Sofia Petrovna's question. "Second Therapeutic Ward?" and then she put down the receiver: "Frolenko, Natalia Sergeyevna, died at four o'clock today without regaining consciousness. Are you a relative? You may have a pass to the mortuary."

15

O<small>N</small> the evening of the nineteenth, putting on her fall coat with a scarf under it, and her galoshes, Sofia Petrovna got in line on the embankment. For the first time she had to stand the whole night through: who could relieve her now? Neither Natasha nor Alik was there any longer.

All alone Sofia Petrovna had accompanied Natasha's pine coffin through the entire city to the cemetery. It rained a long time that day and the great wheels of the horse-drawn cart splattered her face with mud.

Natasha lay in her grave in the yellow earth not far from Fyodor Ivanovich. But where were Alik and Kolya?

She stood on the embankment all night long, leaning up against the cold parapet. Damp cold rose from the Neva. Here for the first time in her life Sofia Petrovna saw the sun rise. It rose from somewhere beyond Okta, and that instant tiny ripples ran across the surface of the river, as if it had been rubbed against the grain.

Near morning Sofia Petrovna's legs went numb from fatigue, she couldn't feel them at all, and at nine o'clock when the crowd made a rush for the doors of the prison, Sofia Petrovna didn't have strength enough to run: her legs had become so heavy she felt she'd have to lift them with her hands to make them move at all.

This time her number was fifty-three. In two hours she was handing money in through the window and giving the last name. The stout, sleepy fellow looked at some sort of card and instead of his usual "not allowed for him" answered "deported." After her conversation with Tsvetkov, Sofia Petrovna was fully

.epared for such an answer, yet all the same the answer stunned her.

"Where to?" she asked distractedly.

"He'll write you himself. . . . Next!"

She went home on foot, because standing and waiting for the streetcar was harder than walking. The dust already smelled hot, she unbuttoned her heavy coat and unwound her scarf. The people passing by seemed to have forgotten how to walk: they kept bumping into her from all sides.

Kolya would write to her. She'd receive a letter again as she had at one time from Sverdlovsk.

All the next several days, without eating breakfast or making her bed, Sofia Petrovna went out looking for work. In the newspapers there were many announcements saying "Typist Wanted." Her legs felt like lead, but she patiently spent the whole day answering every advertisement. Everywhere they asked her the same question: Have you anyone who's been repressed?

The first time she didn't understand. "Relatives arrested," they explained.

She was afraid to lie. "My son," she said.

Then it turned out there were no vacancies on the staff. And there wasn't one anywhere for Sofia Petrovna.

She was now afraid of everyone and everything. She was afraid of the janitor, who looked at her indifferently yet at the same time severely. She was afraid of the house manager, who had stopped nodding hello to her. (She was no longer the apartment representative; the wife of the accountant had been elected to replace her.) She was mortally afraid of the wife of the accountant. She was afraid of Valya. She was afraid to walk by the publishing house. Returning home after her fruitless attempts to find work, she was afraid to look at the table in her room: perhaps a summons from the police would be lying there? Perhaps they were already summoning her to the police station to take her passport away and send her into exile? She was afraid of every ring of the bell: perhaps they'd come to confiscate all her belongings.

She was afraid of handing over money for Alik. On the evening before the thirtieth, when she was making her way to the line, Kiparisova came up to her. Kiparisova appeared almost every day at the line, not just on her day, so she could find out from the women if anything new had happened. Who had been sent away? Who was still here? Had the schedule perhaps been changed?

"You shouldn't do that, not at all!" Kiparisova whispered in Sofia Petrovna's ear when she told her why she'd come. "They'll connect your son's case with his friend's—and nothing good will come of it. Article 58, paragraph 11, counterrevolutionary organization. . . . What do you need to do that for, I don't understand!"

"But they don't ask who's handing over the money," said Sofia Petrovna timidly. "They only ask who it's for."

Kiparisova took her by the hand and led her away from the crowd of people.

"They don't need to ask," she whispered. "They know everything."

Her eyes were huge, brown, and sleepless.

Sofia Petrovna returned home.

The next day she didn't get out of bed. There was nothing to get up for any longer. She didn't feel like getting dressed, pulling on her stockings, or putting her feet over the edge of the bed. The untidiness of the room, the dust didn't bother her. She didn't feel hungry. She lay in bed, without thinking, without reading. Novels hadn't interested her for a long time now: not for a moment could she tear her mind away from her own life and concentrate on somebody else. The newspapers filled her with a vague terror: every word in them was the same as the ones in that issue of the wall newspaper "Our Way". . . . Once in a while she would throw off her quilt and sheet and look at her legs: they were huge and swollen as if filled with water.

When the light had left the wall and the evening had begun, she recollected Natasha's letter. It was still lying under her pillow. Sofia Petrovna wanted to read it again, and propping herself on her elbow, she drew it from its envelope:

"Dear Sofia Petrovna," the letter began.

Don't cry about me, no one needs me anyway. It's better for me this way. Maybe everything will turn out all right and

Kolya will come home, but I don't have the strength to wait. I can't make sense of what's going on right now under the Soviet regime. But you must go on living, dear one, the time will come when it will be possible to send him parcels and he'll need you. Send him canned crab, which he loved. I kiss you warmly and thank you for everything and for your words of support at the meeting. I regret that you had to suffer because of me. You will have my tablecloth to remind you of me. What a good time we had at the movies, do you remember? When Kolya returns, put it on the table for him, the colors on it are bright and cheerful. Tell him I never believed anything bad about him.

Sofia Petrovna put the letter back under her pillow.

"Maybe I should tear it up? She writes about the current phase of the Soviet regime. What if they find the letter? Then they'll connect Kolya's case with Natasha's . . . Or perhaps I should keep it? Natasha's already dead anyway."

16

THREE months went by, then three more—winter arrived, January, the anniversary of Kolya's arrest. In a few months it would be the anniversary of Alik's arrest and right after that the anniversary of Natasha's death.

On the anniversary of Natasha's death Sofia Petrovna would go visit her grave. But on the anniversary of Kolya's arrest there was nowhere to go. Where he was, no one knew.

There were no letters from Kolya. Sofia Petrovna checked the mailbox five times, ten times a day. Sometimes there'd be newspapers for the wife of the accountant in the mailbox or postcards for Valya—from her numerous beaux—but there was never a letter for Sofia Petrovna.

It was already the second year that she didn't know where he was nor how he was. Maybe he was dead? Could she ever have imagined that a time would come when she wouldn't know if Kolya were dead or alive?

She was now working again. An article by Koltsov in *Pravda* had saved her from dying of starvation. A few days after the article appeared—a remarkable article about slanderers and opportunists harming honest Soviet people for nothing—Sofia Petrovna was offered a job at a library: not a permanent job, a temporary position, but nonetheless a job. She had to write out cards for the catalog file in special librarian's script: four hours a day, a hundred and twenty rubles a month.

At her new job Sofia Petrovna not only talked to no one, she didn't even say hello or good-bye. Bending over a table piled high with books, her short gray hair falling down over her glasses, she sat out her four hours, then got up, stacked her cards a pile, took the rubber-tipped cane which always stood beside her chair, locked her cards in the cupboard, and slowly walked out without looking at a soul.

A whole column of canned crab was already mounting up on the window sill in Sofia Petrovna's room, grains of buckwheat crunched beneath her feet, yet every day after work she went around to food shops to buy still more provisions. She bought canned food, rendered butter, dried apples, lard—there was plenty of all these things in the shops, but maybe just at the moment Kolya's letter arrived, one thing or other would disappear.

Early in the morning sometimes, even before going to work, Sofia Petrovna would wander along Obvodny Canal to the old clothes market. There, after bargaining fiercely, she bought a hat with earflaps and some wool socks.

In the evenings, sitting in her untidy, unheated room, she would stitch bags large and small out of old rags. They'd come in handy when the time came to make up a parcel. Plywood boxes of all sizes poked out from under her bed. She ate practically nothing—only drank tea with a little bread. She didn't feel like eating, and anyway she had no money. The food for the parcels was expensive. To economize she heated her room only once a week. And for that reason she always sat at home in her old summer coat and wool cufflets. When she was really cold, she would get into bed. There was no point in cleaning a cold room—it was cold and uncomfortable anyway—so Sofia Petrovna gave up sweeping the floor and only flicked the dust off Kolya's books, the radio and the cogwheel.

Lying in her bed, she would think about her next letter to Comrade Stalin. Since Kolya had been taken away, she had already written three letters to Comrade Stalin. In the first she had asked him to review Kolya's case and have him released since he was not guilty of anything. In the second, she had asked to be told where he was so that she might go there and see him just once more before she died. In the third, she implored him to tell her one thing only: was Kolya alive or dead? But there was no answer. . . . The first letter she had simply dropped into the mailbox, the second she had sent by registered mail, and the third, with a return slip for confirmation of delivery. The return slip came back after a few days. In the space "signature of recipient" was an incomprehensible scribble, in small letters: ". . . eryan."

Who was this "Eryan"? And had he given Comrade Stalin the letter? After all the envelope had been marked: "Personal and Private."

Regularly, once every three months, Sofia Petrovna went to one of the legal advice bureaus. It was pleasant to talk with the defense lawyers—they were courteous, unlike the prosecutors. There was a line there, too, but not much of one, no more than an hour or so. Sofia Petrovna would wait patiently, seated in the narrow corridor, leaning both hands and her chin on her cane. But she waited in vain. No matter what defense lawyer she saw, they all politely explained to her that, unfortunately, there was no way to help her son. Now if his case had been brought up for trial . . .

Then one day—it was exactly one year, one month and eleven days after Kolya's arrest—Kiparisova appeared at Sofia Petrovna's room. She entered without knocking, and breathing heavily, sat down on a chair. Sofia Petrovna looked at her in amazement: Kiparisova was afraid of Ivan Ignatyich's case being linked up with Kolya's, so she never came to see Sofia Petrovna. And now all of a sudden she had come, sat down, and was sitting there.

"There've been some releases," she said hoarsely, "people are being released. Just now in line, with my own eyes, I saw a man who'd been released come to get his documents. He wasn't emaciated, only his face was very white. We all crowded around him, asking: 'How was it there?' 'All right,' he says."

Kiparisova looked at Sofia Petrovna. Sofia Petrovna looked at Kiparisova.

"Well, I'll go now." Kiparisova stood up. "I've got a place in line reserved for me at the prosecutor's office. Please, don't see me out so no one will see us together in the corridor."

They were letting people out. Some people were being let out. They were coming out through the iron gates into the street and returning home. Now they might release Kolya, too. The bell would ring and Kolya would come in. Or no, the bell would ring

…d the mailman would come in: a telegram from Kolya. After all Kolya's not here, he's far away. He'll send a telegram from somewhere on his way.

Sofia Petrovna went out onto the landing and opened the door of the mailbox. Empty. Empty as could be. Sofia Petrovna stared for a moment at its yellow side—as if hoping her stare could call forth a letter from the box.

She had barely returned to her room and threaded her needle (she was stitching up another bag), when the door to her room opened once again without a knock, and the wife of the accountant appeared in the doorway with the house manager at her back.

Sofia Petrovna stood up, her back guarding the pile of provisions.

Neither the nurse nor the house manager greeted Sofia Petrovna. "Look at that!" rapped out the nurse, pointing at the kerosene can and the primus. "Please take notice: she's set up a whole kitchen in here. Soot, filth, she's smoked up the entire ceiling. She's destroying household order. Seems she doesn't want to do her cooking in the kitchen with everybody else— she's scorned us ever since we found her systematically stealing the kerosene. Her son's in a camp, exposed as an enemy of the people, she herself has no fixed occupation, in short, an unreliable element."

"You, Citizeness Lipatova," said the house manager, "take the cooking equipment to the kitchen immediately. Or else I'll report you to the police . . ."

They left. Sofia Petrovna took her primus, kerosene can, strainer and pots back to their old place in the kitchen, then lay down on her bed and burst out sobbing.

"I can't stand it any more," she cried out loud. "I can't stand it any more." And then all over again syllable by syllable in a shrill voice, not holding back at all: "I can-not, can-not stand it an-y-more."

She pronounced the words as earnestly and insistently as though someone stood before her claiming that, on the contrary, she could easily take more.

"No, I cannot, I cannot, I can't possibly stand it any more."

The wife of the policeman came into her room.

"You mustn't cry," she whispered, wrapping Sofia Petrovn̈
in her blanket. "Now, listen to what I'm going to say. Wha͟
they're doing isn't legal. My husband says that since you've
not been deported, no one has a right to bother you. You
really mustn't cry! My husband says they're releasing lots of
people now—with God's help, Nikolai Fyodorovich will soon
return . . . That daughter of hers is getting married, so mama's
got her eye on your room. But just don't move, that's all. The
mama's after it for her daughter, and the house manager, for his
girl friend. So let them fight over it. . . . You really mustn't cry!
It's true what I'm telling you."

17

IN winter almost no street sounds reached her room through the double windows. Sofia Petrovna could, however, hear rustlings and creakings in the apartment all night long. There was the persistent gnawing of mice (if only they wouldn't get into the bacon she'd bought for Kolya). The floorboards in the corridor creaked, and when a truck passed nearby, the front door rattled. And the clock in the accountant's apartment chimed importantly every fifteen minutes.

Kolya would soon return. That night Sofia Petrovna no longer doubted that Kolya would soon return. Kiparisova said so and the policeman, Degtyarenko. . . . He had to return, because if he didn't, she would die. If they were beginning to let innocent people out, that meant they'd let Kolya out soon, too. They couldn't let others out and not Kolya. Kolya would return—and then how ashamed that nurse would be! And the house manager. And Valya. They wouldn't dare to look him in the eye. Kolya wouldn't even say hello to them. He'd walk past them as if they didn't exist. When he came back, they'd give him a responsible job somewhere immediately—even a medal of honor—to make amends for the wrong they'd done him. There'd be a medal on his chest, and he wouldn't even say hello to the nurse and Valya . . .

Toward morning Sofia Petrovna fell asleep and woke up late, at ten o'clock.

When she woke up she remembered: something good happened yesterday, she'd learned something good about Kolya. Ah, yes, they'd started to let people out, that meant soon Kolya would return, and Alik. Everything would be fine, the way it used to be. Sofia Petrovna caught herself thinking: then Natasha, too, will return.

No, Natasha would not return.

But Kolya—Kolya was already on his way home, perhaps his train was already pulling into the station.

Returning home from the library that day, Sofia Petrovna stopped in front of the window of a commission store and stood there for a long time. In the window was a Leica camera. Kolya had always dreamed of owning a camera. Suppose she sold something and bought Kolya the Leica to celebrate his return. Kolya would soon learn how to take pictures—he was so handy, picked things up so quickly.

All day Sofia Petrovna felt happy and elated. She even felt like eating—the first time in many days. She sat down in the kitchen to peel some potatoes. If she did get the camera for Kolya, then there'd be the problem of where to develop them. A completely dark room was necessary. Why, of course, the store-room. There was wood there, but a place could be cleared. She could carry a part of her wood, little by little, into her room and ask Degtyarenko's wife to carry a bundle into hers—she wouldn't refuse—and then there'd be room. Kolya would take pictures of everybody: Sofia Petrovna, the twins, and young ladies he knew—only Valya and the nurse he'd never, on any account, photograph. He'd put together a whole album of photographs, but Valya and the nurse would never appear in it.

"Do you have much firewood in the storeroom?" Sofia Petrovna asked Degtyarenko's wife, when she entered the kitchen for a broom.

"About three bundles," answered Degtyarenko's wife.

"Do you like having your photograph taken? I loved it when I was young, by a good photographer, of course . . . You know what? Kolya's been released."

"You don't say!" exclaimed Degtyarenko's wife, dropping her broom. "So you see, and you were killing yourself!" She kissed Sofia on both cheeks. "Did he send a letter or a telegram?"

"A letter. I've just received it. Registered," answered Sofia Petrovna.

102

"I didn't hear the postman come. You can't hear a thing wit. these primuses going."

Sofia Petrovna went back to her own room and sat down on the sofa. She needed to sit somewhere quiet, to recover from her own words and grasp their meaning. Kolya's been released. They've released Kolya. Looking back at her from the mirror was a wrinkled old woman with dirty-gray hair streaked with white. Would Kolya know her when her returned? She stared deep into the mirror until everything began to swim before her eyes and she could no longer tell which was the real couch and which the reflection.

"You know, my son's been released. From prison," she said to the woman who worked at the library with her, writing out cards at the same table. Until this moment she'd never heard a single word from Sofia Petrovna, and Sofia Petrovna didn't even know her name.

"Well, now!" answered her co-worker, a fat, untidy woman, whose clothes were all sprinkled with hair and cigarette ash.

"Your son was probably not guilty of anything, and so they released him. People in our country aren't kept in prison when they've done nothing . . . Was your son in prison a long time?"

"One year and two months."

"Well, they looked into the matter and released him," said the fat woman, putting down her cigarette and starting to write.

That evening, the policeman Degtyarenko bumped into Sofia Petrovna in the corridor and congratulated her. "You'll be throwing a party," he said, shaking her hand and smiling broadly. "And when will Nikolai Fyodorovich be coming to see his mama?"

"He'll put in a month or two at the factory, and then go to the Crimea for a rest—he badly needs a rest!—and then he'll come to me. Or perhaps I'll go to him," answered Sofia Petrovna, astonished herself at how easily she was saying all this.

She was happy and excited, she even walked faster. And she wanted to go around telling people all the time: "Kolya's been released. Did you hear? They've released Kolya!" But there was no one to tell.

Later that evening she went out to buy bread and ran into the polite accountant from the publishing house. Just the day before she would have crossed to the other side of the street if she had seen him because anything connected with her job at the publishing house was painful to her. But now she smiled at him from afar.

He bowed gallantly and asked at once: "Have you heard our news? Timofeyev's been arrested."

"What?" gasped Sofia Petrovna. "But he . . . But it was he who exposed all the . . . saboteurs . . ."

"And now someone's exposed him . . ."

"You know, I have good news," Sofia Petrovna hastened to tell him. "My son's been released."

"Ah! Allow me to congratulate you. I didn't even know your son had been arrested."

"Yes, he was, but now he's been released," said Sofia Petrovna gaily and bid the accountant good-bye.

When she got home, she automatically looked in the mailbox. Empty. No letter. Her heart sank, as it always did when she saw the box was empty. Not a line for a whole year. Surely it must be possible to smuggle a letter out through someone? A year and two months without any news from him. Was he dead? Was he alive?

She lay down on her bed and felt she'd never get to sleep. Then she took some Luminal, a double dose, and fell asleep.

18

"I received another letter today," Sofia Petrovna told them the next morning in the kitchen. "Imagine, the director of the factory named my son his assistant. His right hand. The Mestkom has procured him a travel voucher for the Crimea—the scenery's gorgeous there, I was there when I was young. And when he returns, he's going to get married. To a young Komsomol girl. Her name's Ludmila—a pretty name, isn't it? I'm going to call her Milochka. She waited a whole year for him, although she had many other proposals. She never believed anything bad about Kolya." Sofia Petrovna glanced triumphantly at the wife of the accountant, who was standing next to her primus stove. "And now he's going to marry her—at once, as soon as he returns from the Crimea."

"That means you'll have grandchildren to fuss over," said Degtyarenko's wife.

The nurse didn't even raise an eyebrow. But a minute later, when Sofia Petrovna came back to the kitchen after going to her room for some salt, the nurse said "good morning" to her as if she was seeing her the first time that day. The first "good morning" in a whole year.

It was Sofia Petrovna's day off and she decided to clean up her room. If Kolya was not free yet, he was bound to be freed any minute now. He'd arrive, and the room was a terrible mess. Glancing at herself in the mirror, Sofia Petrovna decided that she simply must begin to wave her hair again. Otherwise it would hang in lank, gray strands.

She pulled some boxes out from under the bed and lit the stove with them. The plywood burned wonderfully, with a cheerful crackle. Sofia Petrovna began deliberating: where could she put all those cans so they wouldn't clutter up the window sill? What did she need so many cans for? When she needed something, she could always go buy it at the store.

She decided to wash the windows and the floor. Her legs ached as usual and she had a pain in the small of her back, but she'd just have to put up with it. She tore up the bags to use as rags.

While the water was heating, she must go shake out the carpet. Sofia Petrovna carried the carpet out onto the landing. Something dark showed through the cracks of the mailbox. Moving heavily, Sofia Petrovna went to get the key.

Inside the box was a letter. A rough pink envelope. "To Sofia Petrovna," she read. Her name was written in an unknown hand. There was no address, no postmark—nothing.

Forgetting the rug on the landing, Sofia Petrovna rushed back to her room. She sat down near the window and opened the envelope. Who could it be from?

"Dearest Mama!" was written there in Kolya's hand, and so dazzled was Sofia Petrovna by the sight of his handwriting, she let the letter drop into her lap.

Dearest Mama!

I am alive and a kind person has promised to deliver a letter to you. How are you managing, and where is Alik, and where is Natalia Sergeyevna? I think of you all the time, my dear ones. It's terrible to think that you may now be living somewhere else, not at home. Mama, you are my only hope. My sentence was based on evidence given by Sashka Yartsev—you remember, the boy in my class? Sashka Yartsev declared that he had persuaded me to join a terrorist organization. And I had to confess, too. But it's not true, we never had any such organization. Mama dear, Investigator Ershov beat me and trampled me, and now I'm deaf in one ear. I've written many appeals since I've been here, but have never received any answer. You must write yourself, saying you are my old mother, and put the facts before them. You know yourself that I never once saw Sashka Yartsev after I left school, since he was studying at a different institute. And he was never a friend of mine at school. They probably beat him badly, too. I embrace you fondly, greetings to Alik and to Natalia Sergeyevna. Mama, you must do something quickly, I won't last long here. I embrace you fondly.

Your son, Kolya

Sofia Petrovna threw on her coat, jammed on her hat and with a dirty rag still in her hand rushed off to see Kiparisova. She was afraid she might have forgotten the number of her apartment and wouldn't be able to find it. She gripped the letter tightly in her pocket. She had left her cane behind and ran along clutching onto walls. She felt her legs giving way: no matter how she hurried, Kiparisova's was still far away.

Finally, she entered the building and, with her last strength, climbed to the third floor. This must be it. Yes, here it was. "Kiparisova, M. E.—Ring once."

The door was opened by a little girl who immediately ran off. Making her way down a dark corridor, past cupboards, Sofia Petrovna pushed open a door at random and went in.

Kiparisova sat there on a trunk in the middle of the room, in her coat and with a cane in her hands. The room was completely empty. Not a single chair or table, no bed or curtains, only a telephone on the floor near the window. Sofia Petrovna sank down on the trunk next to the old woman.

"I'm being deported," said Kiparisova, showing no surprise at the appearance of Sofia Petrovna and not even greeting her. "I leave tomorrow morning. I've sold everything and leave tomorrow. My husband has already been deported. For fifteen years. You see, I've already packed. I've no bed, nothing to sleep on, I'll sit up all night on the trunk."

Sofia Petrovna handed her Kolya's letter.

Kiparisova sat reading it for a long time. Then she folded it and shoved it into Sofia Petrovna's pocket.

"Let's go into the bathroom, the telephone's in here," she whispered. "One mustn't talk about anything near the telephone. They've inserted some kind of special gadget in the phone and now you can't talk about anything—every word you say can be heard at the exchange."

Kiparisova led Sofia Petrovna to the bathroom, fastened the hook on the door, and sat down on the edge of the tub. Sofia Petrovna sat next to her.

"Have you already written the appeal?"

"No."

"Don't write it!" whispered Kiparisova, bringing her huge eyes, ringed with yellow, close up to Sofia Petrovna's face. "Don't write one for your son's sake. They're not going to pat you on the back for an appeal like that. Neither you, nor your son. Do you really think you can write that the investigator beat him? You can't even think such a thing, let alone write it. They've forgotten to deport you, but if you write an appeal—they'll remember. And they'll send your son farther away, too . . . And who brought this letter, anyway? And where are the witnesses? . . . And what proof is there? . . ." She looked around the bathroom with wild-looking eyes. "No, for God's sake, don't write anything."

Sofia Petrovna freed her hand, opened the door and left. Exhausted but still hurrying, she made her way home. She needed to lock herself in, sit down and think things over. Should she go to Prosecutor Tsvetkov? No. Should she go to the defense lawyer? No.

She pulled the letter from her pocket and threw it on the table, then took off her coat and sat down by the window. It was getting dark and in the gathering dusk streetlights were coming on. Spring was on its way, how late darkness fell already. She had to decide, she had to think—but Sofia Petrovna only sat by the window, thinking of nothing.

"Investigator Ershov beat me and trampled me . . ." Kolya still wrote his "d's" with an upward loop. He had always written them that way even though Sofia Petrovna had taught him when he was little to make the loop go down. She had taught him to write herself. Following specially ruled lines.

It was now completely dark. Sofia Petrovna stood up to turn on the light, but couldn't for the life of her find the switch. Where was the switch in this room? She fumbled along the wall, bumping into the furniture which she'd moved out of place to clean the room. She found it. Then immediately caught sight of the letter. It lay creased and crumpled on the table.

Sofia Petrovna took a box of matches out of a drawer. She struck a match and lit a corner of the letter. It burned, slowly turning to ash, coiling up into a tube. It curled up completely and burned her fingers.

Sofia Petrovna threw the flame on the floor and stamped on it.

Leningrad, 19 November 1939–February 1940

Afterword

[The best description of what happened to *Sofia Petrovna* after it was written appears in Lydia Chukovskaya's book *The Process of Expulsion*, which chronicles her expulsion from the Writers' Union in 1974. This excerpt, translated from the Russian edition published in France in 1979 by YMCA-Press, makes an appropriate afterword to the novella itself. Happily, however, it need not remain the last word. In 1988, nearly fifty years after she wrote *Sofia Petrovna*, Lydia Chukovskaya finally got her wish—the book was published in her own country. In February 1988 the novella appeared in the Leningrad literary magazine *Neva*, and it will soon appear in book form in the Soviet Union as well.—Translator]

In December 1962 fortune truly smiled upon me. The publishing house Sovietski Pisatel (Soviet Writer) signed a contract with me for my beloved book: the novella *Sofia Petrovna*. It is a tale about 1937, written in the winter of 1939–40 after two years of standing in line outside prisons. It's not for me to judge its artistic value, but the value of accurate testimony is indisputable. To this day (1974), I know of no volume of prose about 1937 written in *this* country and at *that* time.

Maybe one exists in some secret hiding place and hasn't yet reached us? Let's hope so . . .

In my novella I tried to show that society had been poisoned by lies as completely as an army might be poisoned by noxious gases. For my heroine I chose not a sister, not a wife, not a sweetheart, not a friend, but that symbol of devotion—a mother. My Sofia Petrovna loses her only son. I wanted to show that when people's lives are deliberately distorted, their feelings become distorted, even maternal ones. Sofia Petrovna is a widow; her son is her life. Kolya is arrested; he is sentenced to hard labor; is called an "enemy of the people." Sofia Petrovna, schooled to believe newspapers and officials more than herself, believes the prosecutor when he tells her that her son has "admitted his crimes" and deserves his sentence, "ten years at hard labor without the right of correspondence." Sofia Petrovna knows full well that Kolya has committed no crime, that he is incapable of it, that to the depths of his being he is loyal to the party, to his factory, to Comrade Stalin personally. But if she is to believe in herself, not in the prosecutor and the newspapers, then . . . then . . . then the universe will collapse, the earth give way beneath her feet, the spiritual comfort in which she has so comfortably lived, worked, rejoiced will turn to dust. . . . Sofia Petrovna tries to believe in her son and the prosecutor at the same time, and in the attempt goes mad. (I expressly meant to write a book about society gone mad; poor, mad Sofia Petrovna is no personal heroine; for me she's a personification of those who seriously believed that what took place was rational and just. "We don't imprison people for no reason." Lose that faith, and you're lost; nothing's left but to hang yourself.)

Sofia Petrovna isn't able to generalize from what she sees and experiences; and she's not to be blamed for that, because to the ordinary person what was happening seemed purposely planned senselessness; and how can one make sense of deliberately planned chaos? Particularly when one is all alone: each person was cut off from anyone else experiencing the same thing by a wall of terror. There were many people like Sofia Petrovna, millions, but when people are denied all documents, all literature, when the true history of whole decades is replaced by fictitious history, then the individual intellect is cast back on itself, on its own personal experience, and it works less well than it should.

. . . For years there was only one copy of my novella: a thick school notebook written in lilac ink. I could not keep the notebook at home: I had already been searched three times and had all my belongings confiscated. A friend gave refuge to my notebook. If it had been found in his possession, he would have been drawn and quartered. A month before the war I left Leningrad for Moscow to have an operation; my friend remained in Leningrad; he wasn't drafted into the army for medical reasons, and as I learned later while in evacuation in Tashkent, he died of hunger at the time of the siege. The day before his death, he gave my notebook to his sister: "Give it back to her—if you both survive."

I survived, and my notebook made it back to me. Then Stalin died and the Twentieth Party Congress took place, and I gave my notebook to a typist for copying, and friends of mine read my story. After the Twenty-second Party Congress, in September 1962, I offered my novella to the Sovietski Pisatel publishing house; everything went according to the rules, proper as could be: in December, after two favorable reviews, the novella was approved, accepted, and a contract agreed to; in January 1963 I was paid sixty percent of my royalty fee; in March I was shown the illustrations already approved by the design department; the manuscript was on the verge of going to press and becoming a book.

Miraculous!

I saw that the publishers were well disposed towards my book, sympathetic to it and to me. The young women editors wept when they read it, and every one asked for a copy to take to mother or husband; the artist completed her illustrations with uncommon speed. So much for the artist! Comrade Karpova herself, the chief editor, the right hand of the director, Comrade Lesuchevsky, that very Karpova from whom up to now in my literary career I'd had nothing but polite crudeness, now addressed me with nothing but crude compliments.

The only thing the publishers asked of me was to write a foreword. I wrote one.

The compliments lavished upon me both sincere and insincere were most understandable. And so also the speed with which my book was read, reviewed, and prepared for press. And why not! After all the "cult of personality" had been unmasked, Stalin's body removed from the mausoleum, and every newspaper, every magazine, every publishing house was obliged to "respond" at least in some degree to "the exposure of the mass infractions of soviet legality"—with an article, a short story, some poetry, a novella, or a novel.

They responded! Karpova, sighing deeply and sympathetically, spoke of the tragic past, unmasked in so wise and timely a fashion by the party—a past that would never return, and of the "restoration of Leninist norms to party life." (As if those norms had been religiously observed in non-party life all along.)

Then suddenly—some sensed it earlier, I, distinctly, in 1963—everywhere, ever-increasing, worrisome rumors began to spread: there'd been a change of course "at the top," dissatisfaction, literature was digging too deeply into the "consequences of the cult," it was time to talk of achievements, not "mistakes"; the party with its decisions at the Twentieth and Twenty-second Congresses had explained and corrected everything; enough is enough. The survivors returning from camps and prisons had been rehabilitated, and not only given housing but, just think of it, provided with jobs; the relatives of those who died had been informed of the posthumous rehabilitation of sons, sisters, husbands; what more did you want? why pour salt on the wounds? let's get on with the latest planting or the latest harvest. "At factory X there's a new blast-furnace."

On 7 and 8 March 1963 explanatory meetings with party and government leaders were held for the intelligentsia. I was not high up enough in the intelligentsia to be invited to such exalted meetings; but in May I received a different sort of invitation, to my publishing house. The head of the department of Soviet literature, Comrade Kozlov, invited me to his office and with apparent friendliness but categorical firmness explained that though accepted, ready for press, and even sixty percent paid for, my novella could not be published.

I wanted to drop in on Karpova upon learning this, but she wasn't there: either she was sick, on holiday, or away on business. I don't remember.

Certainly, the decision not to publish my book was a personal disaster, a cause for grief, but I didn't hold the publishing house to blame. I saw that many of the people who worked there sincerely wanted to publish my novella. After all in our country (in cases of any importance), it's not the editors who decide what to publish or not publish. An order's an order, a forbidden topic's a forbidden topic. . . . However, after a while I did drop in on my book's chief admirer, the main editor of Sovietski Pisatel, Comrade Karpova. I took a seat in an armchair across from her. Did she think, I asked, that the prohibition would last a long time.

"It's strange," I said by the way. "It's like making a decision to publish three novellas, three narrative poems, three short stories, three novels about the Great Patriotic War*—period. 'We're not going to pour salt on the wounds!' But after all every family lost either father, or husband, or brother, or son, and sometimes four people in one family were killed, and it's painful for relatives to remember those who perished. The war lasted four years, but 'the cult of personality' and its 'consequences,' almost thirty. In each family all trace of father, or husband, or brother, or wife, or sister, or sometimes the whole family itself has disappeared. The war was a terrible thing, but one can understand the reasons for it, the idea behind it, but understanding the idea and reasons for 'the cult of personality,' and everything this 'cult' gave rise to, is much more difficult. So every document is precious for future generations, for researchers, my novella included."

"From the very start," Karpova answered as if by rote, "I told you your novella was ideologically flawed. The reasons for and consequences of the cult have been adequately explained by the publication of party documents in the papers. The speeches of Nikita Sergeevich and the meetings for the intelligentsia with party and government leaders have further clarified things. I was never mistaken about the flaws in your position."

Karpova, the chief editor of Sovietski Pisatel publishing house, was famous and is still famous in literary circles for her pathological dishonesty. "To lie like Karpova" became proverbial long ago. But meeting a direct, bold, shameless lie, no matter how often it happens, always stuns one anew. Karpova had never uttered a single word about my book being ideologically defective. Quite the contrary, she more than anyone had hastened to sign the contract and announce the "approval" of the book.

---

*The Russian name for World War II. (Translator)

115

"You should be ashamed of yourself," I burst out.

"Be grateful," Karpova answered, pointing to some papers, "that the publishing house has not demanded its money back. It's a waste to spend government money on your novella."

(Government money! It wasn't for money I wrote my book at a time when all around me in my beloved city every tenth person was being shot, maybe every fifth.)

However, the liar had given me a wonderful thought. The idea for a way to strike back.

"The money?" I asked, getting to my feet. "You don't have the right to ask me to give the money back. It's against the law. A manuscript which has been accepted and readied for publication must be paid for in full. It's not I who owe you money, but you who owe me. I'm going to take the matter to court. The publishing house changed its mind? Then let it pay the penalty, what's the author got to do with it?"

"Just go ahead and try," answered Karpova to my retreating back.

After a time I went to the lawyer for the Writers' Union. When he heard that my manuscript had been approved and accepted, that the illustrations had been done, and that I'd been paid sixty percent of my fee, he determined that I definitely had grounds to sue. But he added: "Writers usually don't sue their publishing houses because the publisher will stop publishing them." That didn't bother me. I went to the Office for the Protection of Authors' Rights where one of the young lawyers, upon acquainting himself with the contract, immediately agreed to prepare a suit on my behalf and to represent me in court.

The time before the trial passed slowly. The judge called me and asked for the manuscript. It took him a month to read it, if not longer. He didn't express any opinion. Then the court date was twice set and twice set aside: the defendant didn't appear. On purpose: or so it seemed to me. Finally, on 24 April 1965, an open session of the People's Court of the Sverdlovsk Region of the city of Moscow took place. The small hall was filled. The judge handled the affair dryly and precisely, as before saying nothing about the novella. The lawyer for Sovietski Pisatel publishing house was very longwinded. He informed the judge that the novella was found to contain "ideological distortion," that at first the publishing house employees, "due to an overzealous response to the Twentieth and Twenty-second Party Congresses," had not noticed the distortion, but now in the light of the new party decisions, "they had looked at the novella with fresh eyes"; that my novella was no more than a photograph of the ugly side of our life; material of the sort which could be used to produce only "a work which struck at clear party positions"; that the novella was ideologically inadequate; that after the publication of *One Day in the Life of Ivan Denisovich* the publishing house had been swamped by a torrent of prison camp books which had to be limited; and as to Solzhenitsyn, he could assure us that no one was about to publish him again. "Yes, yes, he's getting ready to do so, but we're not . . ." "We ourselves didn't realize the danger of the theme, but it was pointed out to us it's not necessary for Communists to publish books on this theme, and even more important, it's not useful . . ." There was laughter and whispering in the courtroom, and I noticed that many people were taking notes.* "If Chukovskaya wins this case," concluded the lawyer for the Writer's Union, "it will set a bad precedent." The lawyer from Protection of Authors' Rights, on the other hand, was very brief. He noted that we were not in England, that legal proceedings in our country were not based on precedent, but the law as to authors' rights was clear (he cited the relevant points): since the manuscript had been approved for publication, the publishing house was obliged no matter what to pay the author the full fee.

The courtroom listened to him sympathetically, the judge, without emotion.

A few times, after one of the speeches by the longwinded lawyer for the publishing house, the judge instructed me:

"Answer!"

I answered. I said, in part, that if they stopped publishing Solzhenitsyn it would be a great shame for the country; that, incidentally, my *Sofia Petrovna* and his *Ivan Denisovich* were novellas written at different times, about different times, and on different themes: his was about the camps, mine, about "or-

*Not long ago I learned that one of the transcripts of these proceedings was published abroad in 1972—seven years later—in *Political Diary*, pp. 51–57. (author)

dinary life''; I also said that if my novella had been accepted and readied for press ''in an overzealous response to the Twentieth and Twenty-second Congress,'' then hadn't it been broken due to an overzealous response to the new moment? And was it possible that the decisions of the Twentieth and Twenty-second Congresses were simply ''an overzealous response . . .'' and nothing more? I said that if the evil done in the past had occurred, wasn't it largely because newspaper editors, snowed under by groaning, weeping, wailing letters in which families beseeched them to investigate the cases of their relatives, had been denied the possibility of printing those letters? The editors were not able to satisfy the demands of the moment. And truly, who at that time ''dared to dare''? To print such a wail would have meant printing your own death warrant.

Wasn't one of the reasons it could happen, the readiness of all editors! across our whole enormous country, the editors of all newspapers, books, magazines, always to obey the baton of the conductor standing in the conductor's stand as to whether to permit some piece of information or other on the pages of his publication (for example, news of illegal arrest and torture)? I said: granted my novella may be only a photograph, not a great painting, but caught on this photograph is a moment of enormous importance to our society, and the novella is essential to all those who wish to think about what took place.

The court assessors* questioned the defendant, mainly clarifying the dates of ''the passage of events.'' The judge was silent. Essentially, he asked the lawyer for the publishing house only one question. Granting him the opportunity to substantiate his assertion that my novella was ''ideologically defective,'' the judge asked:

''Is it true that when the manuscript was approved for publishing and the author was paid sixty percent of her fee the novella was satisfactory?''

Having listened to the lawyer for the publishing house, to the lawyer from ''Protection of Authors' Rights'' and to me, the court withdrew to deliberate.

---

*Two civilians who, together with the judge, hear cases in a Soviet court and serve as jury in the determination of the verdict. (Translator)

Twenty minutes passed:

"The judge enters . . . All rise . . ."

In cautious anticipation, the courtroom rose.

"In the name of the Federated Russian Soviet Socialist Republic . . ."

In the name of the Russian Republic the People's Court of the Sverdlovsk region resolved: the publishing house must pay the author the entire royalty fee since the manuscript had been rejected after it had been approved for publication.

In a few days I received the money . . .

As to the novella?

Courts have no jurisdiction over the publishing of books.

The novella, snapped up by Samizdat long before and traveling hand-to-hand, crossed the border.

In 1965 in Paris the novella was published in Russian by five Continents Publishers under a different name (*The Deserted House*) and with changed names for many of the characters as well (for instance, Olga Petrovna instead of Sofia Petrovna). Then it was published in America, also in Russian, in two issues of *Novy Zhurnal* (New Journal, No. 83 & 84, New York, 1966) under the correct title and without changed names. Then it seems it was translated into many of the world's languages: with my own eyes I have seen it in English, in German, in Dutch, in Swedish and have heard that there are editions in still other languages.

I am grateful to Samizdat, to the foreign publishers and translators. No random search in connection with case No.27 or 227 or 20227 can now destroy my testimony. Certainly it was wrong to give my novella a different title (*The Deserted House* instead of the name of the heroine); my book deals with an educated society driven to loss of consciousness by lies. Sofia Petrovna (Olga Petrovna also) represents this society. The change of title in this case is an attempt to change the basic idea . . . But for all that, I'm still grateful.

However, despite my gratitude, I'm not consoled. There's only one thing I want, just one thing I'm waiting for: to see my book published in the Soviet Union.

In my own country. In Sofia Petrovna's country.

I have been waiting patiently for thirty-four years.

There is but one tribunal to which I wish to offer my novella: that of my countrymen, young and old, particularly the old, those who lived through the same thing which befell me and that woman so different from me whom I chose as the heroine of my narrative—Sofia Petrovna, one of thousands I saw all about me.

EUROPEAN CLASSICS

ଈ

Honoré de Balzac
The Bureaucrats

Heinrich Böll
And Never Said a Word
End of a Mission
Irish Journal
The Train was on Time

Lydia Chukovskaya
Sofia Petrovna

Aleksandr Druzhinin
Polinka Saks · The Story of Aleksei Dmitrich

Konstantin Fedin
Cities and Years

Marek Hlasko
The Eighth Day of the Week

I. Grekova
The Ship of Widows

Ignacy Krasicki
The Adventures of Mr. Nicholas Wisdom

Karin Michaëlis
The Dangerous Age

Andrey Platonov
The Foundation Pit

Arthur Schnitzler
The Road to the Open